Steal My Heart

BACHELORS & BRIDESMAIDS (#2)

BARBARA FREETHY

Steal My Heart
© Copyright 2014 Barbara Freethy
ALL RIGHTS RESERVED

For information contact: barbara@barbarafreethy.com

Chapter One

Screams filled the air as the roller coaster paused at the top peak, allowing the occupants one shattering look at the death drop below. Then the cars went screeching over the edge, defying gravity and risking death. Liz Palmer let out a breath as she watched the speedy descent of the roller coaster called *Shoot The Moon*. She wasn't even on the ride, but she felt her stomach tie itself into a knot that didn't loosen until the frightening screams turned into shaky laughter and the wheels came to a grinding halt along the bottom platform.

She couldn't imagine wanting to ride something so terrifying. She preferred the solid ground beneath her feet, security and stability and things that she understood—not this land of make-believe and illusion. But none of that mattered. She'd come to Playworld for work, not for fun.

The amusement park had opened three months earlier on the outskirts of Sacramento, a ninety-minute drive from her home in San Francisco. Now that their initial launch was over, the Playworld Corporation was looking for a PR firm to come up with a strategic campaign to propel the park into the top tier of amusement parks around the world. She was planning on winning the multi-million dollar account for her company: Damien, Falks and Palmer.

Turning away from the ride, she headed toward the large castle in the center of the park that housed the executive offices. Her heels clicked against the pavement and as she made her way past rides, food concessions and gift shops, she felt decidedly overdressed in her dark gray skirt, cream-colored top and black heels.

She pulled open the sturdy door leading into the castle. Her shoes immediately sank into shaggy dark green carpet that reminded her of walking through grass.

As she made her way to the reception desk, she couldn't help noticing that the playful atmosphere of the amusement park extended to the offices. The walls were covered with impressionistic paintings that looked like dreams, nightmares or fantasies. The furniture was just as fanciful: oddly shaped tables carved out of wood, enormous chairs that would make anyone feel small and mirrors at every angle that seemed to magnify the entire experience. She was beginning to feel like she was in *Alice in Wonderland.*

A perky young receptionist dressed in something akin to a princess costume looked up with a cheerful smile as Liz approached the front desk.

"Can I help you?" the woman asked.

"I'm here to see Mr. Hayward. Liz Palmer from Damien, Falks and Palmer." She pushed her business card across the counter and offered her usual professional smile.

"He's in a meeting at the moment, but I'll let him know you're here. Why don't you have a seat? He should be free soon."

Liz nodded, walking over to one of the chairs with a wary expression. The seat resembled the lap of a friendly giant. There were sleeves on the arms of the chair and the back had a round, cheery face above a bulging chest. Shaking her head in amazement, she sat down, jerking abruptly to her feet when a buzzer sounded. The mouth of the giant opened, and he began to speak. "Hello. I'm Lawrence. Please take a seat. I want you to be comfortable."

Liz looked around the room, wondering if she was going completely crazy. The receptionist was tied up on the phone and didn't appear to be the least concerned with her. Bending down, she took a closer look at the face. Yes, there was a speaker and there were lines where the mouth had opened. She sighed. A talking chair—just what she needed. Maybe she'd just stand.

"Mr. Hayward is free," the receptionist said a moment later. "His office is through those double doors, down the hall, second door on the left."

"Thank you." Liz walked toward the doors, relieved to get down to business.

"Oh, one more thing," the receptionist called out after her. "Watch out for the quicksand. It's Mr. Hayward's idea of a joke. It's pretty clearly marked, but sometimes people miss it."

"Thanks for the tip." Liz walked cautiously into the hallway. It looked normal. The brown carpet appeared to be solid. Had the woman been kidding? Or was she missing something?

A door down the hall opened and a man stepped into the corridor. She was about to give him a brief, impersonal smile, but when her eyes met his, her heart stopped in shock. The man was tall, with light brown hair streaked with gold. His eyes were very blue, and his smile was not only filled with amusement, but was very, very familiar.

Michael Stafford? What the hell was he doing here?

No answer came to mind, but it was definitely Michael. It had been nine years since she'd seen him at their high school graduation. His face was older now, his shoulders broader than she remembered, but the nose she had once broken was still a little crooked.

Why him? Why now? She needed to be on her game, and

Michael had always been one to throw her off balance.

"Lizzie?" he questioned. "Is that really you?"

"Michael?" She took a few steps forward and the floor suddenly fell away. With a startled scream, she fell into a shallow pit.

Michael covered the distance between them in barely a second. "Are you all right?"

"What happened?" she asked in bewilderment. She was now surrounded by pillows, which thankfully had prevented an injury.

"You fell into the quicksand. Didn't they warn you out front?" Michael reached out a hand to help her back up. "The squares are shaded a darker brown here, and there's a sign on the wall, although you practically need a magnifying glass to see it."

She climbed out of the pit as gracefully as she could in a straight-fitting skirt. "Why do I get the feeling I just wandered into the fun house?"

His smile widened. "I don't know. Are you having fun?"

She didn't know how she felt. Her heart was racing, her palms were sweating, and she felt really warm.

"You've grown up nicely," Michael said, his gaze traveling down her body. "Still blond, but I think I miss the long, thick braid and the glasses that made you look so smart and intimidating."

She certainly looked better now than she had in high school, and there was a little part of her that liked the gleam of appreciation in his eyes. "Contacts and a new hair stylist," she said. "Time has been good to you, too." He definitely looked attractive in his dark jeans and light blue button-down shirt. "I have to admit I never thought I'd see you again."

"I recently came back to Northern California."

"Are you living here in Sacramento?"

"No, I have a place in Berkeley. What about you?"

"San Francisco. My parents are still down in Palo Alto, in our old neighborhood." She paused. "Your folks sold their house after we got out of high school, didn't they? I wondered what happened to them."

"They got divorced. My dad moved back east, first to Minneapolis, then Miami and more recently Denver. My mom ended up in Colorado. That house in Palo Alto was the one they owned the longest—five years."

"I didn't realize they'd divorced. Sorry."

He shrugged, then tilted his head, giving her a thoughtful look. "You don't happen to be in Public Relations, do you?"

"As a matter of fact, yes."

"Just like your father." He nodded. "I should have put the two together. But when Mr. Hayward mentioned Damien, Falks and Palmer, I assumed it was your dad."

"My father recently retired."

"So you work for his company now, and you're going after the Playworld account?"

She frowned, her stomach tightening again. "Yes. How did you know that?"

"I'm your competition."

"You're a football player," she said, shaking her head.

"I *was* a football player." Shadows filled his gaze. "I wrecked my knee last year and had to reinvent myself."

"In Public Relations?" she asked in surprise and dismay. "Why?"

"My older sister Erica has a small firm and suggested I join forces with her. I didn't have a lot of other options, so I said yes."

"Well." She didn't know what else to say. She was still reeling from not only the fact that she was standing really close to him, but also because he appeared to once again be her competitor. "Playworld is a big account. If your firm is small, you won't be able to handle the business."

"I can handle anything," he said with his usual confidence. "And frankly, I think Playworld would prefer working with an imaginative, creative PR firm that didn't start in the dark ages."

"And I think Playworld would prefer working with a firm that knows how to run a huge campaign," she retorted.

He smiled. "This takes me back to high school when you and I were both running for student body president."

She didn't care for the reminder, especially since Michael had won. "This isn't high school, nor is it a game."

"Life is a game, Lizzie."

"Liz," she corrected. "And I'm sure you and I aren't the only competitors."

"No, but we're probably the top two."

"You have an ego that doesn't quit. My firm has been in business for forty years, Michael."

"I know. That's why I referenced the dark ages. But it doesn't matter how you start or how hard you play, it only matters how you finish."

"Is that a football metaphor?"

"It's a fact. And I'm glad your firm is my rival. I like to know my competition."

She shook her head against that assumption. "You don't know me. It's been nine years since we've seen each other. We've both changed."

"Probably. It will be interesting to see how we compete now that we're no longer teenagers."

Knowing that Michael Stafford was going to be her competition did not make her as happy as it apparently had made Michael. Past experience told her that whenever Michael was around, things usually didn't go the way she had planned. But this wasn't school anymore, this was business—and her job was on the line.

She squared her shoulders and lifted her chin. "I'd better

find Mr. Hayward. It was nice to see you again, Michael."

"I'm sure we'll be seeing more of each other."

She had the terrible feeling he was right.

* * *

As Liz disappeared into Charlie Hayward's office, Michael blew out an amazed breath. *Lizzie Palmer—what an unexpected surprise.*

Over the years, he'd often wondered what had happened to his female nemesis, the only girl in school who had made him mad as hell and just as hot. There was no reason she should have gotten him that worked up. She wasn't his type at all. She wore thick glasses, pulled her hair back in a braid, and she'd had braces on her teeth for most of the four years they'd been in school together.

As the high school quarterback, he'd had his pick of the pretty, popular girls, but damn if he hadn't spent a lot of time thinking about pulling off Liz's glasses and kissing the hell out of her smart mouth. He had tried to kiss her once, and she'd hit him so hard she'd broken his nose.

He shook his head at the memory. This potential job was getting more interesting by the minute.

In truth, he wasn't as confident about getting the account as he'd let on to Liz. He was still learning the PR game, and there was a big part of him who thought his older sister had bit off more than she could chew by opening a firm with only a few years of experience under her belt. But Erica had pulled him out of a dark place by inviting him to be her partner, and he had always liked a challenge. Maybe his dream hadn't been to run a PR firm, but sometimes dreams died.

Shaking off the gloomy thought, he walked down the hall and out of the building, then took out his phone. Erica was waiting for a report. If they could snag the Playworld account, they'd be set. They could hire more people, invest in bigger office space, really build up the firm, but first, they had to win over Charlie Hayward, and that might just take a Hail Mary.

One advantage he had was that Charlie was a big football fan, and he liked the idea of a celebrity leading the charge for his amusement park. That was one advantage Michael had over the other firms, and he intended to use it.

"How did it go?" Erica asked as she picked up the phone.

"Not bad. Hayward spent a lot of time talking about some of my big plays."

"That's good news. Live off the glory days as long as you can, Michael. Did you find out who we're competing with?"

"Hayward didn't tell me, but I ran into one of our rivals on my way out the door, Liz Palmer from Damien, Falks and Palmer."

Erica groaned. "Really? I didn't think they'd go for an amusement park. It's not really their style."

"They'll change their style for a multi-million dollar account."

"Who did you say was representing them?"

"Liz Palmer."

"Didn't you—"

"Go to high school with her? Yes. Her dad was one of the founding partners of the firm, and from what I know of Liz, she's going to fight hard to get this account. That woman does not know how to quit."

"But you know how to beat her, right?"

He thought about that for a second. "I used to have a good idea of her weaknesses, but we're not in high school anymore."

"Then it may be time to renew your friendship."

"I wouldn't say we had a friendship. We were more enemies than anything else. At any rate, Charlie wants me to get up close and personal with his amusement park. I'm going to need to spend the next few days riding every ride in the park."

"Well, it's a tough job, but someone has to do it," she said dryly.

"You could have made the pitch with me."

"No, you're our front guy. You're good at meetings, I'm better at the actual work."

"I'll be back in the office in a couple of hours, and we'll go over our strategy. I really want to get this account, Erica."

"It would be a tremendous win," Erica agreed.

As he hung up the phone, he couldn't help thinking that Liz Palmer had always brought out the best in him, pushed him harder than he pushed himself. Beating her would make the win that much sweeter.

* * *

"I'm sorry, could you repeat that?" Liz asked, realizing she'd lost track of what Charlie was saying. Her mind had drifted back to the unexpected meeting with Michael. She could not let him distract her.

Charlie Hayward gave her a contemplative look. "Something on your mind, Miss Palmer?"

"No. I just want to make sure I know exactly what you want."

"What I want is for you to get to know my amusement park—ride every ride, eat at every concession, visit every gift shop and exhibit. Only then, will I trust you to put together a promotional plan. You know I built this place for my wife. We dreamed up this park when we first got married, and it took us forty years to make it happen."

The passion he had for his park was evident in his voice and in his brown eyes. Charlie was in his mid-sixties, balding and freckled from the sun, his waist showing a beer gut, but right now he looked like a kid in a candy store. She was touched by his commitment to a dream he'd had his entire life. How many people worked that hard and that long to make something amazing happen?

"We want to see the park packed by Memorial Day weekend," he continued. "That gives you a little over six months to make sure the world knows the kind of magic we have here."

She was happy that he was gearing up for the next summer season. While Internet promotional opportunities were abundant immediately, the more time they had, the more exposure they would be able to get in the print publications. "I completely understand, and I'm excited to put together a campaign for you."

"Good. As I said before, I want the people who work for me to really understand this place. That didn't happen with the last company we worked with, but I was too busy getting everything working and open that I didn't pay enough attention to what they were doing. That changes now. I want this year to be all about promotion."

"I understand."

"I hope so. Frankly, I wouldn't have invited your firm to participate if it wasn't for your father. We were in Rotary together for years, and I was always impressed with his intelligence and vision. I was sorry to hear he was ill. I hope he's feeling better."

"He's hanging in there."

"Well, hopefully your father passed on some of his creative ideas to you."

"He taught me a lot," she said.

"Good. But your father isn't making the pitch you are, so you have to believe in this place as much as I do. Then you have to convince me." Charlie leaned back in his chair. "There are three other firms that will also be giving me a bid. You each have something different to offer. Your company is very well known, highly respected and solid. But you're also expensive, so I'm going to take a look at the discount firm represented by Ed Hoffman. Christa Blake's firm specializes in amusement and hotel facilities, but they may not have the connections I want with the press. And finally Michael Stafford is new, hungry and has a celebrated name. You'll have a battle ahead of you."

"I'm not afraid to fight."

"Excellent. I've arranged to have you all stay at the hotel next door for the weekend. You'll be provided with a week's worth of passes to the park. I'd like to hear your initial proposal next Thursday."

It was only a week, but she could make that work. "I'll plan to move into the hotel tomorrow morning."

"Perfect. Check with the receptionist out front. She'll give you the passes and anything else you need." He stood up. "I'll give you one tip, Miss Palmer. Be creative, be bold and take risks. I don't like to play it safe."

"I'll keep that in mind." She paused as she got to her feet. "Are there any other surprises I should be looking for on the way out? More quicksand, perhaps?"

Charlie laughed. "If I told you what they were, they wouldn't be surprises."

Chapter Two

Three hours later, Liz walked into her small office at Damien, Falks and Palmer. Her father had founded the company almost forty years ago with his friends Howard Damien and Bill Falks. Since then the firm had grown into a huge business and occupied two floors on the thirty-first and thirty-second floor of one of the tallest skyscrapers in San Francisco. However, while Howard, Bill and numerous other account executives occupied the luxurious floor above hers, she'd been relegated to a windowless office by the bathrooms eight months earlier when her father had decided to retire. His latest bout of chemotherapy had left him too weak to keep working. His partners had made no secret of the fact that with her father gone, they were interested in taking the firm in a new direction—a direction that might not include her.

But Damien and Falks needed a reason to fire her, and she did not intend to give them one. She had promised her father she would protect his interests in the company he loved so much. And she would have a much easier time of actually keeping that promise if she could bring in the Playworld account. Thankfully, because of his relationship with her dad, Charlie Hayward had been unwilling to deal with anyone at the firm but her, so she had an edge there. But she was going to need more than an edge. She was going to need a win. If she could bring the account to the agency, the partners would not be able to ignore her.

Her cell phone rang and she smiled as Andrea Blain's name flashed across the screen. Andrea was one of her closest friends and several weeks ago, her normally career-obsessed friend had fallen in love. Tonight they were all getting together to celebrate Andrea's birthday.

"Hi Andrea, what's up? You're not calling to cancel, are you?"

"No, just to change the venue," Andrea replied. "I was thinking pizza party at my place."

"Really? You don't want to do anything more fancy for your birthday?"

"No. What I really want to do is spend time with my girls, and we never have enough time to talk in a crowded restaurant. Laurel is bringing the pizza, Kate and Julie are bringing wine, and Isabella is going to do a salad."

"What can I bring?"

"Veggies or chips and dip...whatever you want. I don't think Maggie will be able to make it. They're shorthanded at the hotel, and Friday nights are tough for her to get away."

"That's too bad. I'm a little surprised you don't want to spend your birthday with Alex though."

"He's taking me away tomorrow for the weekend," Andrea said happily. "Knowing Alex, it's going to be spectacular and over the top."

"I agree. I think you found yourself a good one, Andrea."

"I know I did. I'll see you at seven, Liz."

"See you then."

As Liz ended the call, a knock came at her door, and Bill Falks walked into the room. She got to her feet, preferring to deal with the partners at eye level, not that she even came close to meeting Bill's eyes. He was at least six-foot-four, and since she was barely five-five, he had almost a foot on her. She had no doubt that he loved to use his height as an advantage.

"Hello, Bill," she said, her tone cool. "What brings you down here?"

"How did your meeting at Playworld go?"

"Quite well. I'll be putting the proposal together over the next few days."

"Howard and I think you might be able to use some help on that."

"I'm good. I know exactly what Charlie Hayward wants."

Bill stared back at her. He knew as well as she did that the firm didn't have a chance in hell of getting the account if it weren't for her father's previous relationship with Hayward. "Liz, this doesn't have to be a fight."

They were talking about more than Playworld; she knew that. She didn't flinch from his hard gaze. "I agree. I just want to do my job and bring the firm a great client."

"That's what Howard and I want as well. I know you think we've been hard on your father, but he's a stubborn man. He sticks to old ideas that have no bearing in this new technological world."

"My father is as technologically savvy as you and Howard are," she said. "I don't know why you were so eager to shove him out when he got sick, but he didn't deserve that."

"We didn't shove him out; he retired. I had no idea you were so angry, Liz."

"Really? You thought moving me downstairs and isolating me from the other senior account executives would make me happy?"

"You weren't the only one to be moved."

No, but the other associates who had been moved had all been at the firm less than a year while she'd been working there for six years, and that didn't count the years in college when she'd been an intern doing every menial task in the company. But she wasn't going to get into all that with Bill; it was pointless.

"Well, I'm sure we'll be able to move you back upstairs once we finish the remodel," Bill said, clearing his throat. "At any rate, let me know if I can be of assistance on the Playworld pitch."

"I'll do that."

As Bill left, she sank down in her chair and blew out a breath. She was twenty-seven years old and Bill had thirty years on her, but she'd held her own. Unfortunately, just holding her own wasn't going to be good enough. She had to get the Playworld account, or her next relocation would probably be out of the building entirely.

* * *

Several hours later, Liz knocked on the door of Andrea's apartment with a veggie tray she'd picked up at the market and a bottle of cabernet. She was about fifteen minutes late, and she could hear laughter and conversation within. Just the sound of those female voices made her feel less stressed. These women were so important to her. They'd met their freshman year in college, sharing a common bathroom in the dorm, and since then had become best friends.

She was expecting Andrea to open the door, but it was Kate Marlowe's sparkling blue eyes that met hers. Kate was a pretty brunette with one of the warmest smiles in the group. A wedding planner, Kate was also the most romantic.

"Liz," she said happily, giving her a hug. "Glad you could make it."

"Me, too," she said, following Kate into the room.

Andrea was on the couch with her twin sister Laurel, a bunch of photographs spread out on the coffee table in front of them. While they were twins, Andrea and Laurel were opposite in appearance. Andrea had long blonde hair and Laurel had light brown hair that fell just to her shoulders.

Across from Andrea and Laurel was Julie Michaels, another attractive brunette. Liz had met Julie in high school and they had been roommates in college. Julie now worked in fundraising for a children's charity, and Liz's firm had actually sponsored one of their recent events, so their professional lives often mixed with their personal lives.

"Hi Liz," Julie said, her mouth pull of pizza. "Sorry, we didn't wait for you to start eating."

"Don't worry. I'll catch up."

"Hey, Liz," Andrea said, getting up from the couch.

"I figured you might need more wine," she said, holding out the bottle.

"Always," Andrea said with a laugh. "And you know I love red."

Liz set the veggies on the coffee table, then followed Andrea into the small kitchen. There were two large pizzas on the counter as well as a big bowl of salad.

As Andrea opened the bottle of wine, Liz aid, "Sorry I'm late."

"No worries. Work?"

"Yes, I had to catch up on a few things before I leave tomorrow."

"Where exactly are you going?" Andrea asked, pouring Liz a glass of wine.

"Playworld Amusement Park."

Andrea raised an eyebrow. "Why? You hate roller coasters. They make you want to throw up. And sometimes you actually do throw up. Remember the *Fearsome Flyer* ride at the boardwalk?"

"Don't remind me," she said with a groan. "My company is competing for the Playworld account, and the owner of the park told me that I have to go on every ride and visit every concession stand before I write up my pitch. That includes the monster roller coasters."

"How are you going to do that, Liz?"

"I have no idea, but I can't let a roller coaster take me down. I need this account. If I can sign Playworld, I'll be bringing in millions of dollars. I'll be able to call my own shots at the firm."

"Maybe get an office with a window?"

She nodded, knowing that Andrea understood office politics better than anyone. "Yes, but that's enough about me. How is Alex and the love story of the century?"

Andrea smiled. "It *is* a pretty fantastic love story, I have to say. I never thought that much about falling in love until Alex knocked me off my feet. I certainly wasn't looking for love when I went to interview him two months ago."

"But that's exactly what you found. It's good to see you happy, Andrea."

"It feels good. Now, I want all of my friends to fall in love."

Liz smiled. "Well, unless Alex has six terrific brothers, that may take some time."

"Unfortunately, he's an only child. Grab some pizza and we'll go join the others. Laurel finally got her wedding albums back from the photographer, and she made up albums for each one of us."

Liz took a slice of pizza and followed Andrea back to the living room.

For the next hour, she ate pizza, drank wine and listened to Laurel talk about her first six wonderful weeks as a married woman. It was fun to see both Andrea and Laurel in love, but Liz was in no hurry to join the happily-ever-after crowd, at least not until she got her career under control.

"Look at this, Liz," Laurel said, holding up a photograph.

"Your expression is hilarious."

Everyone laughed at Liz's shocked look as she caught Laurel's wedding bouquet.

"I thought you were going to throw it to Andrea," she said defensively.

Laurel gave a helpless shrug. "I was trying. But I guess I was stronger than I thought."

"So this means you're the next bride," Kate said.

"I'm going to have to find a man first," she said dryly.

"Is there anyone you're interested in?" Julie asked.

She hesitated as Michael Stafford's image flashed through her mind.

"There is someone," Kate said, jumping on her pause with a question in her eyes. "Who is it?"

"It's no one."

"You were thinking of someone a second ago," Kate said. "So talk."

"I was thinking of someone, but he's not a love interest."

"Who are we talking about?" Andrea asked.

"A guy I went to high school with."

Julie straightened. "Our high school? Who?"

"Michael Stafford."

Julie's eyes widened. "The high school quarterback? The guy that beat you out for student body president and pretty much everything else you ran for?"

"That's him. I ran into him today at Playworld. He's no longer a pro football player. He apparently runs his own public relations firm, and he's competing against me for the Playworld account."

"Just like old times," Julie said with a gleam in her eyes. "Michael used to really annoy you. I don't think I ever heard you rant about anyone the way you did about him."

"He's still annoying."

"Is he still hot?" Julie asked.

"He's all right," she muttered, seeing the smiles spread across her friend's faces. "I am not interested in him. He's a rival. I don't want to date him. I want to beat him."

"You will," Julie said confidently. "He's a football player. He can't be as good as you are, not in the world of PR."

"I hope not," she said, but she couldn't help thinking that underestimating Michael Stafford had been her downfall before. She would not make that mistake again.

Chapter Three

Liz walked through the gates of Playworld just after ten on Saturday morning. She'd already checked into the adjacent hotel and was eager to start her research. It was certainly a nice day for a trip to the amusement park. Despite the fact that it was mid November and Thanksgiving was only a week away, the temperature was already around seventy degrees.

She stripped off her sweater and tied it loosely around her waist, then paused in front of a large map to get her bearings.

The park had been built in the shape of a teddy bear, another sign of Charlie's insane desire to replicate every childhood fantasy. Each part of the bear provided a different experience, and she considered her options. She could take a ride on a roller coaster, spend some time under the sea or rocket through outer space. She could visit worlds of nightmares and fantasies without ever closing her eyes, or go back in time to the wild, wild West and the jungles of prehistoric man. Danger and adventure lurked around every corner.

She sighed, wishing she had the thrill-seeker gene, but she'd never loved the idea of heart-pounding, palm-sweating, stomach-dropping excitement. Maybe she could work her way up to the big rides, start with something easy.

Turning her back on the screeching cars of the roller coaster, she walked toward the carnival game section. Throwing darts at balloons, she could handle.

As she walked toward the first booth, the attendant gave her the typical carnival call. "Step right up," he sang out. "Bust the clown's nose and win a prize."

It wasn't his words that made her stop, but the sight of Michael Stafford preparing to throw a dart at a large clown's nose. The clown face was whirling around on a fast wheel, making the challenge that much more difficult. Dressed in faded jeans and a t-shirt, he looked like the guy from her youth, and her heart unexpectedly skipped a beat.

Michael tossed his dart and just missed the nose. A large buzzer went off. Michael frowned. "I thought I had that one."

"Try again," the attendant said. "You might get lucky this time. Only two dollars for five more tries."

As Michael dug into his pocket for his wallet, his gaze caught on Liz. Too late, she realized she'd lost her chance to slip away.

"Lizzie," he said cheerfully, waving her over. "Have you tried this one yet?"

"I just got here."

"Then it's your turn. My treat."

"I can pay my own way."

"Relax, it's two bucks," he said, handing the money to the attendant. "And I took it out of the cash Charlie left for us."

She nodded. "All right then." While most of the rides in the park were included in the entrance fee, the games here were set up like a true carnival, cash games with stuffed animals as prizes.

Michael handed her the five darts. "Here you go. I have to tell you it's harder than it looks."

"I'm surprised you would say that. You're a quarterback. You should know how to throw something at a target."

"You'd think," he said dryly.

She looked back at the spinning wheel, took aim and launched her first dart. It missed the clown's face entirely, way too short of a throw.

"At least I hit the target," he said mockingly.

"I'm getting warmed up."

She tried again. Her next three shots struck various parts of the face and head but came nowhere near the nose. She was down to her last dart, and she had the really strong feeling that beating Michael at this simple game would set the tone for the rest of the week. She picked up her dart and tried to time the spinning wheel.

"You might have to accept that you're not good at everything," Michael said.

She frowned. "You're trying to distract me."

"Just preparing you for disappointment."

"I don't plan on being disappointed."

"You always were overconfident."

"That was you, not me." She focused her gaze back on the clown, drew her arm back and threw towards the target. She was almost as shocked as Michael was when the clown's nose burst and bells rang.

"A winner. We have a winner here," the attendant shouted, drawing the attention of a group of nearby tourists. "Step right up. Everybody wins."

"I don't believe it," Michael said in unhappy surprise. "You got lucky."

"If that's what you want to think. Which prize would you like? The pink panda or the yellow bunny?"

"Very funny."

"I think I'll take the pink panda. It will go with your red face."

"Try again, lady, you can win the lion," the attendant advised.

"I'll stick with the panda." She tried to hand it to Michael, but he crossed his arms in front of his chest.

"No, thanks. You won it; it's yours," he said.

"Are you sure? I'm happy to share because…well, because I won."

A smile curved his lips. "I forgot about your tendency to gloat."

She could have told him that it wasn't possible he'd forgotten, because she had never had the opportunity to gloat. Back in high school, she couldn't remember a time when she'd actually beaten him. Hopefully, the panda was a sign of things to come. She smiled back at him. "What's next? Maybe we can find a game you'll do well at."

He laughed. "You're different, Lizzie. I don't remember you laughing much in school."

"Probably because I wore braces for six years."

"Your teeth look perfect now."

"They should. My parents practically had to mortgage the house to get them in this condition."

"How are your parents?"

Her smile faded at his innocent question. "Actually, my dad is battling cancer."

"I'm sorry," he said quickly. "I didn't know."

"Why would you? Anyway, he's a fighter so we're hoping for the best."

"You must get your fight from him."

"I think so. What about your parents? I know you said they were divorced, but are they well?"

"Yes, everyone is healthy. "My dad is still working, still traveling, very caught up in his new wife and his new life. My mother has become a quilting fanatic. I now have enough quilts to last me a lifetime, but it seems to keep her busy, and she loves being creative."

"That sounds nice. Has she remarried?"

"No, I think it pains her a little to see my dad with his much younger wife, but what can she do? Luckily, we don't run into him all that much."

"That's a drag. I can't imagine my parents breaking up. That would be really hard."

"I'm a little surprised you ended up working for your dad's firm. What happened to your art, Lizzie?"

His question sent a wistful zing down her spine. Her art seemed like a very long time ago. "It was just a hobby."

"You were really good. I remember that mural you painted in the front hallway of the school. It was amazing. I always thought you'd do something with art."

"It's hard to make money with art," she said. "My dad really wanted someone to go into his company. My brothers weren't going to follow in his footsteps. Tom is a dentist and Greg is an accountant, so it was up to me."

"Why did anyone have to follow in his footsteps? Why not follow your own dream?"

"I like what I'm doing," she said defensively. "And I'm good at it."

"I don't doubt that. But it's not your passion—is it?"

"Does it matter? I know PR is not your passion."

"True, but I went after my dream. Unfortunately, it ended on an operating table."

"Do you miss football?" she asked, seeing the shadows in his eyes.

"A lot," he admitted. "Especially now that it's football season again. It was easier not to think about it during the off season."

She could understand that. She felt a wave of compassion for his far-too-short career. Michael had been a great football player. It was sad that he couldn't play anymore. And she was getting way too friendly with him, she realized. She needed to get her focus back. "I should get going."

"Where are you headed?"

"I thought I'd go to the theater and hear Charlie's story."

"I'll go with you."

She wanted to send him on his way, but there was no danger in watching the movie together. After that, she'd go it alone. She had no interest in revealing her fear of roller coasters to her competition.

On the way to the theater, they passed a mom dealing with a squealing toddler who was apparently very unhappy about something. Liz paused. "Any chance your little girl would like this panda?" she asked.

The girl's sobs immediately quieted.

"Thank you," the mom said with heartfelt sincerity. "She just dropped her ice cream cone, so this helps a lot."

Liz smiled and handed the girl the bear.

"That was nice of you," Michael said.

"I thought she needed it more than I did."

Five minutes later they sat down together in a small theater of about two-dozen seats. There were no other guests in the auditorium, so they took seats in the middle of the second row.

"This attraction doesn't seem to be bringing in the crowds," Michael commented.

That was certainly true. And being alone with Michael in a dimly lit theater now didn't seem like the brightest idea. "Maybe we should come back later."

"It says it's starting in five minutes. Might as well get this task out of the way."

"I guess."

"So do you see any of the old crowd from high school?" he asked.

"Just Julie Michaels. We ended up being college roommates. I don't know if you remember her."

"Sure," he said with a nod. "Her father was a baseball

star."

Of course Michael would remember that about Julie. "He was," she agreed. "But not a star at being a husband or father. He cheated on her mother," she added at his questioning look. "And he had another kid with his long-time lover. It was really hard on Julie. I don't think she even talks to him anymore."

"That's rough," Michael said.

"Not an uncommon story when it comes to pro athletes," she murmured.

He met her gaze. "No, but then it's not really an uncommon story at all, is it?"

She shrugged. "There's more temptation when you're young, rich and an athlete. Surely, you would agree with that. You must have had tons of groupies following you around."

"I had my share."

"You don't have to pretend to be modest, Michael. Don't forget I was there at the beginning of your stardom. You had groupies when you were in high school."

He gave her a speculative look. "You sound a little annoyed, Liz. What exactly is your problem with me—besides the fact that I beat you at everything you tried to do?"

She frowned. "I didn't like your attitude back then. Everything came so easy for you. You didn't even care about the things you were beating me at; you just liked to win."

His gaze filled with surprise. "How do you know I didn't care?"

"I could tell. You were all about football and cheerleaders. You only ran for student-body president on a whim. It wasn't like you wanted to make the school better."

"I was a good president, Liz. And I think you have a chip on your shoulder because you always lost to me."

"Whatever. I don't know why we're talking about this," she added, waving her hand in the air. "High school was a million years ago."

"Not quite that long. We have our ten-year-reunion coming up next spring."

"I will not be going to that."

"Why not?"

"Because I like my life now. I don't need to be reminded of the past."

"What about seeing your friends?"

"I see Julie all the time, and my friends now are mostly college or work friends. They know the real me, not that girl in high school who tried too hard."

He nodded, studying her with far too much concentration.

"What?" she asked. "Why are you staring at me?"

"You didn't like yourself much in high school, did you?"

"I don't know. High school was high school," she said with a shrug. "Does anyone really like themselves then? Well, maybe you did, because you were super popular. The guys loved you. The girls loved you. Even the teachers loved you. I think your experience was quite different from mine."

"Not all the girls loved me. When I tried to kiss one of them, she punched me in the face and broke my nose."

She stiffened at his words. "I was hoping we weren't going to talk about that."

"Why did you hit me, Lizzie?"

"Because you were kissing me as a joke."

"What makes you say that?"

She stared at him in astonishment. "What makes me say that? You were you, and I was me, and your friends were all standing around at that party ready to make fun of me."

"I never intended to make you feel like you were a joke," he said, a serious note in his voice. "That kiss was an impulsive idea, I admit. But it wasn't a premeditated act. I didn't gather everyone around and say watch this. I don't even remember who was around. I just remember how pretty you looked that night. You'd finally taken your hair out of that damn braid."

Her stomach turned over at his words, and the insecure high school girl that still lurked inside her liked the idea that he'd thought she was pretty.

Was he lying?

Maybe he was trying to charm her. Perhaps this was part of his plan to throw her off her game.

"Let's not talk about the past anymore."

"I need an apology first. You broke my nose."

"Fine. I'm sorry about that, but I still don't think your motives were as pure as you're making them out to be."

"Then it's my turn to say I'm sorry I gave you that impression. So, truce?" He held out his hand.

She sighed and put her hand into his. "Truce."

His warm fingers curled around hers, and he held on far too long. Her heart started to beat a little faster and for a moment—just a moment, she had the crazy idea he might kiss her again. Then the lights in the theater went out, and music began to play.

Michael let go of her hand and she shifted in her seat, directing her attention to the movie. She should be grateful for the interruption. She needed to refocus on what was important to her and her father and her firm, and that was getting this account, not reconnecting with Michael Stafford.

Charlie's smiling face came across the screen. He talked about the dream he and his wife had had when they were both barely twenty years old. Through marriage, kids, and several jobs, they made money and saved money until they could bring their dream to life. It took forty years, but it just went to show that no dream is ever too old to come true.

The video went on to show the construction crews breaking ground, the creation of the roller coasters, and the fantasies behind many of the games and rides. Charlie Hayward had certainly been a visionary, a man willing to put everything on the line for his dreams. How many people were really willing to do that?

She was beginning to understand that this park wasn't just a business for Charlie; it was the culmination of years of hard work.

A few minutes later, the film ended, and the lights went back on.

They made their way outside, pausing on the theater steps.

"That was more inspiring than I thought it would be," she said. "I have a lot of respect for Charlie. He built his dream."

"Yeah, he did that," Michael muttered, but there was something about his expression that made her curious.

"What are you really thinking?"

He hesitated and then said, "I was thinking that some dreams aren't under our control."

"You're talking about football."

"Actually I'm done talking about football. So what's next? Should we shoot the moon?"

His mention of the giant roller coaster made her realize that she needed to get rid of him now. "I'm going to fly solo," she said.

"Why? It's not like either of us are going to give away any secrets or strategies while we're riding the rides. And it might help both of us to see the park through someone else's eyes."

"Today I want to concentrate on my own vision."

"All right," he said reluctantly. "Why don't we meet in the hotel bar for drinks around five? I'll invite our other competitors to join us."

"They're not going to come."

"Of course they will. Surely, you've heard the expression 'keep your enemies close'."

"Is that what you're doing with me?"

He laughed. "No. You, Lizzie, are in your very own

category."

"I'm not going to ask what that means. See you later."

"Have fun."

She would have fun, she told herself, but as she walked away, she already found herself wishing she'd stuck with him a little longer.

Chapter Four

After a long day of too many tourists, too much sun, and too many stomach-turning rides, Liz took a shower, changed into a nice pair of black slacks and silky top and made her way to the bar at the Portman Hotel. She paused in the doorway looking around the dimly lit room. A burst of laughter from the far table caught her attention, and one swift glance determined it was Michael and two other individuals. He'd made good on his promise to get the other competitors together, which didn't make her feel any better about having him as a rival. He was already proving to be a better strategist than her by simply inviting his opponents to get closer so he could assess their strengths and weaknesses.

She'd catch up, she told herself.

Walking across the bar, she couldn't help thinking how attractive Michael looked. His hair was damp as if he'd just gotten out of the shower, his cheeks smoothly shaven, and as she got closer, she caught the seductive musky scent of his cologne. But it was his blue eyes and the sexy smile that undid her.

Damn! All he had to do was look at her, and butterflies started dancing in her stomach. She needed get a grip.

"Lizzie," he said, getting to his feet. "Glad you could

make it."

"Sorry I'm late."

"We're only on the first round. "Do you know everyone?"

"Actually, I don't."

Michael waved his hand toward the slender brunette sitting next to him. "Christa Blake from the Morrison Group and Ed Hoffman from Sharp Enterprises. Lizzie Palmer, from Damien, Falks and Palmer."

"Actually, it's Liz," she corrected, shaking Ed's hand.

Ed was a middle-aged man with glasses and a serious expression. He was dressed in tan slacks and a polo shirt. Christa appeared to be in her early thirties and wore a red clingy dress that showed off her great body.

"I know your father," Ed said. "I heard he was ill. I hope he's on the mend."

"He's doing his best to get there," she said, taking a seat between Christie and Michael.

"Can I get you a drink?" Michael asked.

"I'll have some white wine."

Michael motioned to the waiter and ordered her drink.

"It's my understanding, Miss Palmer," Ed continued. "That your firm is doing some reshuffling. I'm a little surprised they sent you here. I would have thought Bill Falks would be handling the account."

"No, it's all mine," she said, determined not to get into a discussion of her office politics.

"Really?" Ed asked doubtfully. "I spoke to Bill last week. He told me that you were considering other career options now that your father is retired."

"You must have misunderstood," she said evenly.

"Perhaps."

She was relieved when the waiter set down her wine, not just because she really needed a drink, but also because she didn't care to discuss her job with her competitors.

"Is Bill Falks still an arrogant asshole?" Christa asked her.

Liz choked on her wine. "Uh, what?"

Christa laughed. "I'll take that as a yes. I worked as an intern at Damien, Falks and Palmer right out of college. Worst six months of my life. I learned a lot, but it wasn't worth having to put up with Bill Falks, who loved to accidentally bump into me and steady himself by putting his hand on my ass."

Liz was a little shocked at Christa's assessment of Bill. But then she'd come into the company as her father's daughter, so even as an intern, she'd never dealt with Bill the way Christa had. Christa was probably six or seven years older than her, too, which meant she'd probably been an intern about the time Bill was going through his midlife crisis and subsequent divorce. Not that that was any excuse for what sounded like bad behavior.

"You ever had a problem with Falks, Lizzie?" Michael asked.

"No, but I don't deal with him that often."

"Lucky you," Christa said. She gave Liz a speculative look. "Do you and Michael know each other? Lizzie sounds like a nickname."

"We went to high school together," she admitted.

"We hadn't seen each other in almost ten years until yesterday," Michael added.

"Well, isn't that fun," Christa drawled. "Did you two date each other in high school?"

"No way," Liz said with vehement shake of her head. "Michael and I were not in the same group."

"What group were you in, Michael?" Christa asked.

"Dumb jocks," he said. "Lizzie was a nerd. Actually, that's not even true. She was an artist, one of those girls who always seemed to have paint on her clothes."

She frowned at his words, wishing she could say they

weren't at all accurate, but she often would get lost in her art project and then the bell would ring, and she would have to run out the door so as not to be late for her next class. Sometimes, the paint ended up on her clothes or hands.

"I was never artistic," Christa said. "Thank goodness we have an art department at our firm so I never have to worry about that."

"We all have art departments," Ed grumbled.

"That wasn't my point," Christa said.

"I'm sorry. But I need to go. I have to study my notes. Thanks for the drink. I'll see you all around."

"You sure you don't want to have dinner with us?" Michael asked.

"I think it best if we keep some distance between us," Ed replied as he got to his feet. "Good luck to you all."

"I guess that leaves the three of us," Michael said. "Want to grab a bite to eat in the hotel restaurant or we could venture away from the park. I know a great Italian place in old Sacramento."

"That sounds lovely," Christa said. "Unfortunately, I have another dinner to go to. Maybe I could have a rain check? I'd love to hear more about your football career, Michael, and how you got into Public Relations."

"Any time," Michael said.

"Nice to meet you, Liz," Christa said, getting to her feet. "I'm sure I'll see you around the park."

"I'm sure you will," Liz agreed.

"And then there were two," Michael said with a grin. "What do you say? Have dinner with me?"

She really needed to say no. It was one thing to have drinks and get to know her competitors and another thing to go out to dinner with Michael.

"Don't say no. You already made me spend the day alone in an amusement park, which is really not that much fun.

You're not going to make me eat alone, too?" he asked.

"I'm sure you could find some company if you tried."

"I'm trying right now."

She couldn't help but smile and give in. "All right, but we split the check, and we don't talk business."

"I can live with that. You can take your time with the wine. There's no rush."

"Actually I'm starving." She drained her glass. "Let's go."

* * *

Valentino's was an Italian restaurant that had the atmosphere of an old speakeasy, starting with a narrow staircase that led down into a basement entrance. The inside of the dining room was decorated with dark wood paneling on the floors and walls. Cozy booths circled the main floor of tables and a rather spectacular bar took up a good portion of the room.

After being seated in a booth lit only by candlelight, they'd ordered dinner and drinks and were now waiting to be served. Liz felt a little more nervous than she should. She'd been out with business associates before, so this should be no big deal, but there was something about the dim lighting and Michael that had her all stirred up. In fact, the way her stomach was churning now reminded her a lot of high school.

"What are you thinking about?" Michael asked, a curious gleam in his eyes.

"I was thinking that I really didn't like you in high school," she said, deciding to go for honesty.

"I know it bothered you that I beat you, but didn't you have any respect for me at all?"

"It's possible that I admired you a little," she conceded. "But that was probably five percent of the time."

"Ouch," he said lightly.

"Sorry. It must be strange to be out with someone who doesn't adore you."

"Actually, it feels like a challenge."

"To change my mind?"

"You don't think I could?"

She shook her head. "Definitely not."

"We're not teenagers anymore, Lizzie. You've changed. So have I. Maybe we should get to know each other as we are now."

He had a point. She waited for their waiter to pour them two glasses of wine, then said, "So who is Michael Stafford now?"

He didn't answer right away. In fact, there was a somber note in his gaze as he took a sip of wine.

"Is it that difficult of a question?" she asked.

"A year ago, I could have answered that question without hesitation, but I'm still figuring things out since my injury derailed my career."

"You seem to move pretty well. I haven't noticed a limp. Is there any way you could go back to playing football?"

"No, I can live a normal life, but I'm done playing professional football."

"I'm sorry."

"Me, too."

"So now you're going to take over the PR world?"

"That's the plan, starting with Playworld."

She sighed. "We're not talking about Playworld tonight, remember?"

"You're the one who brought it up."

"And I'm shutting it down. No business talk."

"Okay." He rested his arms on the table as he leaned forward. "Do you still paint, Lizzie?"

She stared back at him, wishing now she hadn't banned the business discussion. It had been over a year, maybe two, since she'd pulled out her paints, and she did miss that part of herself. "I haven't in a while."

"Why not?"

"Just busy with other things. Let's get back to you."

"My favorite subject," he joked.

She couldn't help smiling at his easy grin. "At least you admit it. Most guys pretend they're interested in listening to my stories when all they're really doing is trying to find a way to get the focus of the conversation back to them."

"Sounds like you've had some bad dates."

"Too many to count. What about you? Do you have a girlfriend?"

He shook his head. "Nope. I'm as single as they come."

"When was the last serious relationship?"

"I don't know that I would have called it serious, but it was a few years ago."

"So you're still living up to your three weeks and you're out rule?"

His gaze narrowed. "Where did you hear that?"

"I think it was after one of the football games. Dana Hamilton, the cheerleader was crying in the corner that you'd dumped her, and one of your friends—I think his name was Robbie—said you had a three week rule, and she should be happy she lasted the whole three weeks."

"Robbie was a douche, and I never had that rule."

She shrugged. "Maybe it wasn't a rule, but you did get around."

"Everyone got around in high school—except maybe you."

She frowned at that pointed comment. "Well, I had more important things to do."

"Always so serious. Do you ever lighten up?"

"All the time. I can be fun."

He laughed. "Yeah, you're going to have to show me that

if you want me to believe you."

"I don't care what you believe, and we were talking about you. I know pro athletes don't have trouble finding women, so what's the story? Why are you still single?"

"Finding women is easy, finding the right woman—much more difficult."

"Maybe you just don't want to commit."

"I have to admit that commitment to a woman has not been at the top of my list the last few years. Or at least I never met anyone that made me want to make it a priority." He lifted his glass to his lips and took another sip. "What about you? When was your last relationship?"

"Senior year of college. I dated a guy for almost two years. But after we graduated, we ended up in different cities and found long distance didn't work. He didn't want to move and neither did I, which pretty much meant we weren't that in love with each other, so eventually we broke up. Since then I've been single in the city."

"Living it up."

She tipped her head at his dry note. "I've enjoyed my life the last few years. And I have a lot of single girlfriends, although they're starting to fall one by one."

"Same with my friends. And once they fall, they want everyone else to fall."

"Exactly," she said. "I had the bad luck to catch the wedding bouquet at my friend Laurel's wedding six weeks ago, and since then everyone has been eager to tell me that I'm going to be the next bride, which is crazy, since I would need at least a boyfriend to make that a possibility."

"I'm sure you could find one. You're a beautiful woman."

Her cheeks warmed at his words. "You're good with compliments, Michael."

"Certainly better than you. You should just say thank you."

"Thank you."

"And you're even prettier when you smile," he added. "I can only imagine what you'd look like if you ever let go of your iron control."

Her nerves tingled as his intense gaze made her wonder exactly what he was imagining.

Thankfully, their conversation was interrupted by the arrival of their entrees.

For the next fifteen minutes they concentrated on their meals and general conversation. Liz asked Michael to tell her a little more about his days as a football player, and his stories about coaches, players, friends and locker room pranks were entertaining. As the minutes passed, Liz found herself falling under the spell of his charm, which alarmed her on a lot of levels. If she could start to like him, even after their past together, how on earth would Charlie Hayward not be just as charmed? She was going to have her work cut out for her to beat Michael on a personal level.

But the pitch wouldn't be personal, it would be about what their firms could do to promote Playworld and she should be able to beat Michael there. He might have been a star football player, but he was a novice when it came to PR. Although it wasn't just him at the company, and she had no idea how good his sister or any of the other employees were. Maybe she should find out.

"Tell me about your sister Erica," Liz said. "She's a couple of years older than you, right?"

"Three years," he said. "She's great. She's very smart and also a sweetheart. She has one of the biggest hearts of anyone I've ever met."

"Is she married?"

"She was engaged to a man she worked with a couple of years ago, but it fell through. She was devastated."

"Did she call it off?"

"He did. He got cold feet. I wanted to kick his ass, but Erica wouldn't let me. She said if he felt that way she'd rather know now than later. It was still a rough year for her. But she bounced back. She threw herself into her work and two years ago, she decided to go out on her own with a guy she met at her previous agency Kent Holcombe. They used their initials to form EK Promotions and they've done really well."

"I've heard of them. They're a small boutique firm."

"Well, that will change when we get Playworld."

She didn't bother to address that comment. "How did you get involved in the agency?"

"Erica felt sorry for me after my injury. I didn't know what to do next, and she said she could use my help at the agency, so I said yes."

"I'm surprised Erica or Kent didn't do the pitch. They have more experience than you."

"Charlie is a football fan."

Her stomach tightened. "Oh, now I get it."

"We divide up the work in the way that makes the most sense," he said. "Don't worry, we know what we're doing."

"I'm sure you do," she said, sitting back in her seat. "I was just curious."

"I'm curious about something, too. Ed made some comments about your firm earlier that I found interesting. Why would your partner tell him you were thinking of leaving?"

"He misunderstood. I'm not going anywhere."

"Have things changed there since your dad left?"

"Definitely. But I can hold my own."

"I have no doubt about that." He paused as the busboy cleared their plates. "Do you want dessert?"

"No, I think I'd like to get back to the hotel. I want to write up some notes before I go to bed." Mostly, she just wanted to end this evening before she started to like Michael even more.

The waiter brought over their bill and several minutes later, they were getting back into Michael's car.

"I really thought you'd drive a Porsche or a Corvette," she said, sliding into the front seat of a dark gray pickup truck.

"Not my style." He'd barely finished speaking when his cell phone rang. He glanced at the screen. "Damn. This guy has been calling me all day. Do you mind?"

"Not at all," she said.

"What's up, Hank?" Michael paused, as the other man took off on what appeared to be a fairly loud rant.

Liz couldn't hear the exact words but the tone sounded a little agitated.

"It's not my problem. I can't help you," Michael said. "I already told you—" He fell silent again as the caller obviously cut him off. "I have a new life now. And it's not football. Fine, I'll think about it. But don't hold your breath."

He ended the call and slid the phone back into his pocket.

"Who was that?" Liz asked, knowing it was absolutely none of her business, but she was quite curious.

"The offensive coordinator for the Arizona Blackhawks," he said.

"Your former team?"

"That's the one."

"What did he want? It sounded like he wanted you to come back. I thought you said you couldn't play anymore."

"I can't play. He wants me to come back as his assistant. Their record is 2-3 and they're trying to turn things around before the season is over," he explained.

"And you don't want the job?"

"No, I'm done with football," he said forcefully. "I need to leave it alone. I have a new career now, and that's where I'm going to put my energy."

"Well, if you're sure…"

He flung her a hard look. "I'm sure."

But as he started the truck and sped out of the parking lot, she wondered if that was really true. Michael had definitely been bothered by the phone call. Even now, he seemed a million miles away. And despite his words, she doubted he was thinking about Playworld or his sister's company; he was thinking about the game that he'd once loved more than anything.

Would he really be able to stay away from it?

She couldn't help thinking that if Michael left his sister's agency, then Charlie Hayward would lose his favorite football player. That could only help her.

But that was a selfish thought, and as she glanced over at Michael and saw the bleakness in his gaze, she knew that he was hurting, and while she wanted to beat him, she didn't really like seeing him in pain. "You can always think about it," she ventured, breaking the silence.

"I already have and I made my decision. This doesn't really involve you, Lizzie. And if you're thinking I might bail and let you have a clear shot at Playworld, you're dead wrong."

"I don't need a clear shot. I know I can give Charlie what he wants."

"So can I."

"But despite your words just now, your reaction to that phone call tells me that while you might know what Charlie Hayward wants in a PR campaign, you don't know what you want to do. You just know what you're *supposed* to do."

"Same thing," he said.

"Is it?"

"Damn you, Lizzie. Why do you always have to challenge me?"

"Maybe because you need the challenge," she retorted.

"Maybe you do, too. We always got better when we had

to beat each other. But let's not forget one important fact. I always won. This time is not going to be any different."

"We'll see about that."

Chapter Five

Sunday morning Liz grabbed an early breakfast, then took the shuttle to the amusement park, arriving just as the gates opened. She enjoyed roaming around the park without a lot of people around. Her first stop took her onto a boat that traveled through the rainforest. She was amazed by the incredible scenery, the sounds of the birds, even the streaming rain that they passed through without actually getting wet. She was impressed with how much thought Charlie had put into every detail, mixing reality with fantasy, technology fueling everything in the hidden background.

As she got off the ride, she took a moment to sit down on a nearby bench and jot down her thoughts. While she had her phone for quick notes, she found herself pulling out a spiral notebook and quickly sketching some of her impressions of the ride. She wouldn't necessarily use the art in her pitch, but it would help her remember the scenes and even the feelings those scenes had evoked.

"Look who's here," Michael said.

She raised her gaze to his, a little tingle of excitement running down her spine at the same time.

He gave her a wary smile. "So last night didn't end on the greatest note. I feel like I should apologize."

"Is that an actual apology?"

"Yes," he said sitting down next to her. "I shouldn't have taken that call while you were in the car. I thought I'd gotten rid of most of my football baggage, but apparently I'm still carrying a few bags around."

She appreciated his candor. "I shouldn't have needled you when you were upset."

"I wasn't upset. I was annoyed."

She had a feeling he'd experienced many more emotions than just annoyance, but she didn't want to get into it with him now.

"You got an early start," he continued.

"So did you."

He looked down at her notebook. "Wow, that's good. Did you just draw that?"

"Yes," she said, quickly turning the page.

"What? Are you afraid I'm going to steal your idea?"

She shrugged. It wasn't so much that she was afraid he would steal something but that she never liked to show her art until it was done. Not that she was creating anything special at the moment. "It's just random doodling," she said. "What have you done today?"

"Nothing much yet. You?"

"Just the rainforest ride. It was amazing. What I love about Playworld is the mix of thrill rides with fantasy. There's something everyone can enjoy. And while there are parts of this place that remind me of other amusement parks, it has its own unique vibe. It's like you walk through the gates and then strip off your adult expectations and become a kid again. Charlie has recaptured that moment where anything feels possible." She stopped abruptly, realizing she'd given a lot away. Clearing her throat. "What are your thoughts?"

"I was thinking along the same lines."

"Great," she muttered.

He laughed. "Lizzie, you don't have to worry. I'm not going to steal anything from you, not art, not ideas, not words. I can come up with my own."

"Well, you might not steal anything intentionally, but this is why we shouldn't go through the park together."

"You don't think I could have figured out on my own that Charlie wants to turn adults into kids when they enter the park?"

"I'm not going to argue with you."

"You used to love to argue with me."

She got to her feet. "I need to keep going. I have a lot of ground to cover."

"I'll be right behind you," he said, standing up.

She sighed. "You're going to follow me, aren't you?"

"Oh, yeah. It was really boring on my own yesterday. I got very tired of holding up one finger when they asked how many in my party. One is definitely not a party."

She couldn't help smiling at his dry comment. She'd felt exactly the same way. It was bad enough to be a party of one at a restaurant but in an amusement park, it felt really weird. "Fine, we'll go together. I was going to hit the speed track next."

"Great. I haven't done that one yet."

She hadn't either, and she didn't think she'd embarrass herself on that ride. She could handle speed. It was flying high and upside down that got to her. Somehow she'd have to get rid of Michael before they got to the roller coasters.

Three hours later, they'd covered all the important rides except one, and Liz found herself staring up at the giant roller coaster.

"Time to shoot the moon," Michael said, an eager light in his eyes.

"I thought you did it yesterday."

"Yeah, but I didn't do it with you."

She glanced down at her watch. "I don't have time today."

"What are you talking about? It's only one. The park doesn't close for hours."

"I know, but I have to drive down to my parents' house. Since my dad got sick, we've made a point of spending Sunday afternoons together."

"Well, there's not a long line. We should be done here in twenty minutes."

"No. You can do it by yourself. I have to go." Before he could try to persuade her to get into line, she took off at a fast pace.

"Hold on," Michael said, jogging up behind her. "What is going on with you?"

"Nothing. I just realized the time, and I need to get home. It's important."

"I get that, but are you sure there isn't more going on? Like maybe you don't want to ride the roller coaster?"

"I will ride it, just not today." She'd force herself on there, but when she did, she didn't intend to have Michael as an audience. "You should go back and get in line," she said, walking again.

"I'll wait and do it with you—maybe tomorrow."

"Sure," she said.

"So your whole family is getting together this afternoon?" he asked, falling into step with her.

"Yes, my brothers and their wives and kids."

"Sounds like fun."

A sudden thought occurred to her. There wasn't much she could do to make her dad's life easier, but maybe there was one thing… "What are you doing this afternoon?" she asked impulsively, hardly believing the words as they left her mind.

He seemed as surprised as she was. "What did you have in mind?"

"Do you want to come with me?"

"Really? What's the catch?"

"No catch," she said. "I can't guarantee it will be exciting in any way, but my mom is making roast beef for dinner."

"I haven't had a home-cooked meal in a while," he said slowly. "But you made it pretty clear you don't like me much. So why the sudden invitation?"

"I don't know. It's not a big deal. You don't have to come. You probably shouldn't come. I'll be taking you away from work."

"Maybe that's your motive."

She sighed. "Forget I asked."

"No, I'm coming."

"Great," she said. She'd tell him about her father's football fanaticism when they got there.

* * *

Michael still wasn't sure why Liz had decided to invite him to Sunday dinner at her parents' house. But he was happy to take a break from Playworld and get to know Liz outside of the competition.

Ever since she'd come back into his life, he hadn't been able to stop thinking about her. She was different than most of the women he'd spent time with in recent years. She had goals and drive, stubborn determination, and a hunger to win. But she was also very attractive with beautiful hair, big brown eyes, and a great body. She'd definitely blossomed after high school. Not that she'd appreciate him telling her so.

She didn't care much for compliments, or at least *his* compliments. For some reason she didn't trust him. Did that mistrust all stem from that one attempt at a kiss in high school? He really hadn't been setting her up for some humiliating fall, but he could see in retrospect that he might have put her in a bad position. But that was a long time ago.

He needed to show her that she could trust him.

Frowning, he wondered why he needed to show her anything. It shouldn't matter what she thought of him. After this promotional competition ended, would they even see each other again?

He found himself wanting the answer to that question to be *yes*.

"You can get off at the next exit," Liz said, interrupting his thoughts.

"Right. It's been a long time since I've been in Palo Alto."

"You've never come back to the old neighborhood?"

"I thought about it, especially after I moved to Berkeley, but I never got around to it."

"Did you like Arizona?"

"It was hot."

She laughed. "The desert can certainly be hot."

"And so much of the landscape was the same. It wasn't me. I liked playing for the Blackhawks, but I wouldn't have minded getting traded to San Francisco. Unfortunately, that didn't happen."

"You're here now."

"Yeah," he said, a sigh following his words.

Liz gave him a look. "Are you thinking about the call you got last night?"

"Yes, and the one I got this morning. Hank is persistent. The Blackhawks are playing San Francisco tomorrow— Monday night football. He wants me to meet him and hear his offer in person."

"Are you going to go?"

"Probably not."

"I don't get why you're so adamant about it. You love the game. If you can't play, why not coach?"

"Because I can't be that close to something I can't have anymore. It would be too hard. All I ever wanted to be from the time I was a little kid was a football player." He paused, thinking back to all the years he'd spent playing the game. "You know that my dad used to travel a lot?"

"Yes."

"So he wasn't a big part of my life. When he was home, I wanted his attention. I didn't really get it until I started to play football. He'd been a football player in college, and he loved that I was following in his footsteps. It was something we had in common. He'd come home from his trips, and we'd head straight to the park to throw the football around." He glanced at Liz. "Those were the best days."

"It's nice that you both shared a love of football." She gave him a thoughtful look. "When is the last time you spoke to your dad?"

"A week after my surgery. So I guess it was last year."

"He hasn't been in touch since then?" she asked in surprise.

"We lost the last link between us."

"If you coach, you might get that link back."

"I don't want it back anymore, not if that's all there is."

"Maybe with time your feelings would change."

"I doubt it. I haven't even been able to watch a football game since I left the Blackhawks. I got caught in a bar once when the channel changed, and when I saw the familiar uniforms, I couldn't get out of there fast enough."

"Oh."

There was an odd note in her voice. "What?" he asked suspiciously.

"This trip might not have been a good idea, Michael."

"Why is that?"

"My dad is a huge football fan. He spends all day Saturday watching the college games and all day Sunday watching the pros. When we get together on Sunday afternoons, we watch the games together. And during halftime, my brothers usually play catch with their kids in the park across the street."

His gut tightened at that piece of information. "You could have told me that sooner."

"I know," she admitted, a guilty look in her eyes. "But I was afraid you wouldn't come."

"And why would that matter? You've been trying to keep your distance from me. Why change that now?"

"Because my dad doesn't have a lot to be excited or happy about lately. He's holding his own with the chemo, but he's had a bad year. There are so few things I can do for him that make any difference in his life, but I know he'd be really excited to talk to you. He's followed your career ever since you got drafted out of high school."

"So you're using me."

She frowned at his suggestion. "I didn't really think of it that way. I just thought he'd love to meet you. You're a hometown hero in Palo Alto. Whenever your name is spoken, it's usually with great reverence."

"Okay, now you're pushing it," he said dryly.

"I'm really not. You know you're a celebrity."

"I *was* a celebrity."

"With sports heroes, you rarely lose the glow of glory, at least with sports fans. Don't be surprised if my dad remembers every big play you ever made, and that would include your college days in Michigan."

"Did I ever meet your dad back when we were in school?"

"I don't think so. He wasn't traveling, but he did work a lot, so he didn't come to many school events. He usually left that to my mom."

"I do remember your mother. She always made those caramel apples for Halloween."

"She still does—every year. She's a great cook. At least you'll have a good dinner tonight."

"That's something." As he stopped at a light, he glanced around the familiar intersection, which was just a few blocks from the high school. He would have turned right to go to his old house. On impulse, he did just that.

"This isn't the way," Liz said.

"Do you mind? I want to see my old house."

He drove down the quiet suburban streets with big, shady oak trees and bits of his past flashed through his mind. He'd only lived in Palo Alto for four years, but they'd been happy years. He'd actually been able to start and finish high school at the same school. And his family had been happy then, at least until graduation.

He pulled over in front of his former house, a two-story three-bedroom home. The yard looked the same. He could still remember popping his skateboard down the three steps off the front porch.

"That's it," he said.

"I know," Liz replied.

"Did you ever come over?" he asked quizzically.

"Of course not. I was not invited to your parties."

"I don't think anyone was invited," he said with a laugh. "People just showed up."

"The cool kids."

He tipped his head. "Probably true. So how did you know where I live?"

"My friends and I threw toilet paper at your house one night."

"That happened about a hundred times," he said with a laugh. "You'll have to be more specific."

"I think it was after one of the dances. In fact, I think there might have already been toilet paper in the trees when we arrived. You were very popular."

"It wasn't fun. I had to clean it up."

"The price you had to pay for being so loved."

"You really hated me, didn't you?"

"I don't know about hate. You just irritated me—a lot."

"I know it looked like I had everything in high school. But that was part of my act. I changed schools a lot and I learned quickly how to make friends and blend in. By the time I got to high school, I was a pro. But it was harder than it looked to come into a new school." He paused. "I used to think the only person who had any idea there was more to me than met the eye was you."

"Me?" She looked at him searchingly. "Why would you think that?"

"Because you didn't look up to me the way the other kids did, and when I ran against you for president of the science club you actually asked me about my views on evolution." He smiled at the memory. "Nobody else thought I could even spell the word, much less explain it. But you actually spoke to me like I had a brain in my head."

"I probably wanted to make sure you were qualified," she replied, offering him a rueful grin. "Or I just asked you that to try and show you up."

"But it didn't work."

"No, it didn't," she agreed. "You actually came up with a credible answer, and I thought good-looking and smart, too. It just wasn't fair."

"So you thought I was good-looking?"

"Fishing for compliments, Michael? That's beneath you. You have a mirror. You know what you look like."

He laughed at her bluntness. "You are one of a kind, Lizzie."

"Because I don't pander to your ego?"

"Because you actually use words like *pander*," he retorted. "Your intelligence is a little intimidating."

"Good. I need every advantage I can get."

Her words reminded him they were in a competition, and

he was taking quite a detour into the past, but as he gazed back at the house, he could still see himself walking through those doors, yelling out he was home, flopping on the couch next to his mom while she watched whatever murder mystery movie was on the television.

"Things were good here," he muttered. "I felt close to my parents in this house. My sister was already in college the last three years, so a lot of times it was just the three of us or just my mom and me. After graduation, everything went to hell. I found out that my parents had wanted a divorce for a while, but they'd waited until I graduated from high school before dropping that bomb."

"I'm sorry, Michael," Liz said, compassion in her eyes.

"Luckily, I had college waiting and football, of course. I should probably be thankful my parents waited until I was leaving the house. I know that they both deserved to be happy, so if being together wasn't going to make them happy, then they made the right decision."

She nodded. "That's a good way to look at it."

He took one last look at the house, then pulled away from the curb. "Let's go see your family."

"I should have told you that I was inviting you to basically a football viewing party," she said. "If you want to drop me off, I can find another way back to Sacramento."

"It's a long drive," he reminded her.

"I can always rent a car."

"No, you're not going to do that. I'm fine. Just tell me there will be snacks."

"More than you could imagine."

Chapter Six

Despite Michael's willingness to come to her house, Liz felt a little guilty about exposing him to the football fanatics in her family. It would be good for her dad, but having heard a little more of Michael's story, she wondered if it would be good for him. He obviously had an emotional attachment to the game, the dream career he'd worked so hard to get and the abrupt collapse of everything he'd ever wanted. She'd always thought of him as the *Golden Boy*, the one for whom everything always went right. But that had certainly ended last year.

Still, he had recovered. He was back on his feet, working for his sister, going after huge PR accounts as if he had all the experience in the world. She really didn't need to feel sorry for him.

Not that she did feel sorry for him. No, her feelings were far more complicated than that.

"Turn left at the next street," she said.

"I remember," he muttered.

Now it was her turn to ask, "How do you remember where I live?"

"I wanted to talk to you after you broke my nose, so I drove to your house."

"But we didn't talk," she said, meeting his gaze.

"No, I chickened out."

Silence followed his words. She knew she should leave it alone, but somehow she couldn't. "What were you going to say to me?"

"That you had it wrong," he said with a sigh. "But you wouldn't have believed me. And I couldn't risk taking another punch to the face. My parents were all over me about what had happened at the party."

"Did you tell them I hit you?"

"God, no! I couldn't tell my father that a girl broke my nose."

She smiled. "My older brothers taught me how to fight."

"They did a good job." He paused. "Did you ever tell your parents?"

She shook her head. "No, it was too embarrassing. I kept thinking I might have to. I waited for you or your parents to call them or to report me to the school. I don't think I slept very well for the next few weeks—if that's any consolation."

"Not really. My nose is still crooked."

"It gives you character. And you played football. I'm sure I wasn't the only one to take a shot at your face."

"I took some hits, but I usually had a helmet and face mask on. And you didn't only leave me with a physical scar, I was a little gun-shy when it came to kissing a girl for months after that."

"I'm sure you got over it."

He parked the car in front of her house, and as they got out, she saw her brothers and their kids at the grassy park across the street. Her oldest brother Tom waved to her, motioning her over. "It must be halftime," she said. "Come and meet my brothers."

Tom came over to give her a hug while Greg threw the football to four little boys who went racing to catch it.

"I wasn't sure you were going to make it," Tom said.

"I told you I'd make the time. This is Michael Stafford," she added as her brother's interested gaze moved to Michael.

Recognition flickered in Tom's eyes followed by excitement. "The football player?"

"Former football player," Michael replied.

"I saw that hit you took on your knee," Tom said. "That was painful to watch."

"Even worse to experience," Michael said lightly. "You look like you have some young football players here."

"Cameron and Doug love to play," Tom said. "Joey and Mark would probably rather be building something, but it's a Sunday afternoon tradition." Tom paused, giving Michael a quick look. "Hey, you wouldn't want to throw the kids a pass, would you?"

"Tom," she protested. "I didn't bring Michael here to play football."

"I know I shouldn't ask, but Cameron is playing peewee football right now, and he hasn't been doing very well. It would really perk him up to meet a pro player."

Liz saw the strain behind Michael's smile and knew she'd put him in a bad position. "Maybe later," she said. "I want Michael to meet Dad."

"It's okay," Michael cut in. "I'd be happy to throw some passes to the kids."

"Great," Tom said, leading Michael over to meet Greg and the kids.

She watched as Michael immediately jumped into the game. He demonstrated the best way to throw the ball, then sent the kids a short distance away so they could practice their catches.

While Tom was helping the kids get into position, her brother Greg came over with a smile.

"Michael Stafford? Dad is going to love you," Greg said.

"Does he know Michael is coming?"

"It's a surprise."

"I didn't know you and Stafford were friends."

"We were in the same grade but not friends. However, I ran into him a few days ago. He's actually competing for the same account. So we're rivals again."

Greg gave her a thoughtful look. "If you're opponents, why are you hanging out with him?"

That was a good question. "I thought Dad would love meeting him."

"Well, that's true. Dad is going to go nuts. He used to rave about Stafford when he was playing for the high school team. I think he wished Tom or I had been even half as good as Stafford, but we did not have the talent." Greg paused. "So now Stafford is in PR?"

"With his sister's firm. He can't play anymore because of his injury."

"That sucks. Good for him for moving on."

Michael was good at moving on, she thought. He was also good at hiding his feelings. She knew the last thing he wanted to be doing right now was playing football with her nephews, but once committed, he'd completely invested himself in the activity. And he was good with the kids, too. He was patient, lighthearted and encouraging. He would make a great coach. Maybe he should really reconsider his stance on the next stage of his career. Not that it was any of her business.

"Look at Cameron's face," Greg said. "He's over the moon."

She saw the adoration in her nephew's face as he looked up at Michael, and it reminded her of how often she'd seen people look at Michael that way. As teenagers, she hadn't been as impressed with him, but seeing him now putting himself out for her family, she had to admit she was starting to like him even more.

Bringing him home had definitely been a bad idea.

Fifteen minutes later, Michael had an even worse idea.

"Let's play a game," Michael said, waving her over. "We need you, Liz."

"I don't think so."

"Come on, Lizzie, Greg said impatiently. "We can do four against four if you play. And you can be on Michael's team."

"You can be my receiver," Michael told her with a cheerful smile.

"Maybe you can be my receiver," she returned. "Or do you only know how to throw a football?"

"I can catch. Can you throw?"

"I can throw," she said, meeting his gaze.

"Well, I want to see that," he returned.

"Then let me show you."

"You're on."

She and Michael lined up with two of her nephews while her brothers faced them with the other two boys.

Her nephew Cameron hiked the ball to her. Michael dodged Greg with a move worthy of an NFL player and headed toward the far end of the park. He wasn't going to make it easy on her, she quickly realized. Sidestepping Tom, who was closing in fast, she drew her arm back and threw the ball to Michael.

It had been years since she'd thrown a football, but it was probably the best spiral she'd ever thrown. She was more than a little pleased to see the shocked look in Michael's eyes when the ball landed perfectly in his hands. He turned and ran toward the designated goal line.

She let out a squeal of delight and ran across the grass. She was going to give him a high five, but as she raised her hand, he grabbed her around the waist and spun her around.

Laughing, he finally set her down. "That was a great pass, Lizzie."

"I taught her to throw," Tom said.

"Wait a second. I'm the one who taught her," Greg complained.

"Well, it doesn't matter, let's see how well you two defend," Tom said.

They lined back up again and for the next twenty minutes they played like the kids they'd all once been. Unfortunately, the game came to an end when Greg's pass sailed over one of the neighbor's fences.

While her brothers bickered about who was going to get the ball, Michael put his arm around her shoulders and said, "Nice throwing, Lizzie."

"For a girl?" she asked, smiling up at him.

"For anyone. You did surprise me. I always thought of you as an artist or a nerd; I had no idea you could play football with the boys."

"Having two older brothers and a father who loved the game made it impossible for me to avoid learning how to throw a spiral. It has been awhile though. I surprised myself. Thanks for playing today. I know it wasn't what you had in mind."

"It was more fun that I thought it would be."

"You're really good with kids. I think my nephews will be raving about you at school all week."

"Your nephews are great, easy to teach, excited to learn. They reminded me of how I felt when I first started to play."

"Well, I know I promised you some snacks, so why don't we go to the house? My father is going to be excited to meet you."

As they walked across the street, Michael kept his arm around her shoulders, and seeing as how he was being so nice to her and her family, she didn't push him away. Plus, she really liked being close to him, and this moment in time wasn't going to last very long, so she would just enjoy it.

The house she'd grown up in was a two-story, three-bedroom home, with a living room and formal dining room that were rarely used. All the real action took place in the big family room where she found her parents. As she'd expected, her father was on the couch in front of the 70-inch TV her brothers had bought him for his last birthday. The coffee table was laden with chips and veggie platters. While her father muttered at the refs about their latest line call, her mom knitted.

Liz smiled to herself at the familiar sight, feeling a comfort in the sameness of it all. Her dad had gone bald with the chemo and he was thinner than he used to be but he still had the fire in his eyes when he cared about something, whether it was football or work, or anything else. He was the one who had taught her to always give a hundred percent, no matter the job, no matter the odds against her success.

Her mother was a fair blonde with short curly hair and a sparkly smile. Her mother couldn't knit anything but blankets, and they all had far more than they could use, but she still kept on knitting. She said it relaxed her and she hated to be idle. The knitting had come in handy during the many long hours she'd spent accompanying her husband to chemo and waiting for tests to come back.

"Liz," her mom said in happy delight, as she caught sight of them. "I'm so glad you came."

"I wouldn't miss it." She licked her lips, realizing her mom's astute gaze had registered the fact that a very attractive man had his arm around her daughter's shoulders. She really should have moved away from Michael earlier. She stepped forward, Michael's arm dropping from her shoulders. "I brought someone I thought you might want to meet. This is—"

"Michael Stafford," her father said, cutting her off. His eyes lit up with excitement as he kicked back the footrest of the recliner and sat up. "I can't believe it. Michael Stafford is in my house. What is going on?"

"Sir," Michael said, moving across the room to shake her father's hand.

"Call me Ron," her dad said. "This is my wife Joan."

"Nice to meet you both," Michael said, giving her mom a warm smile.

"You, too," Joan said. "Please sit down. Liz didn't say she was bringing any visitors."

"I wanted it to be a surprise," she said.

"Can I get you anything?" her mother asked as Michael took a seat on the couch.

"I'd love something to drink," Michael replied. "I worked up a sweat playing football across the street."

"Really?" Joan asked, giving Liz a quizzical glance.

"We ran into Greg and Tom," Liz said. "They wanted to play a game with Michael, and he was nice enough to say yes."

"It was fun," Michael said. "I had no idea Liz knew how to throw a spiral."

Her dad nodded. "She was actually better than Tom and Greg. Don't tell them I said that."

Michael laughed. "I saw that at the park."

"Do you want a beer?" Liz asked.

"That sounds great."

"And I'll get more snacks," Joan added, following Liz out of the room.

Liz walked into the kitchen and smiled at her sister-in-law Amber and her six-year-old niece Hannah. They were covered in flour with sheets of cookies ready to be put in the oven. Amber was married to Tom. "What have we here?"

"Auntie Liz," Hannah said, sliding off the counter stool to come over and hug Liz. "We're making cookies."

"I can see that. Are any done yet?"

"You'll have to wait about twelve minutes," Amber said.

"Did you happen to see my husband on your way in?"

"Yes. But Tom and Greg are trying to figure out who is going to knock on the Colemans' door to get the football back."

"Tom threw that ball over the Colemans' fence again?" her mother asked with annoyance in her eyes. "That must be the hundredth time."

"This time it was Greg," she said, wiping a smudge of flour off Hannah's face "And even though he's thirty-two years old, Greg is still afraid of 'mean old man Coleman'".

"He's not mean, just depressed," her mom said.

"I guess." She opened the refrigerator door and pulled out a beer.

"So Amber, Liz brought home a man," Joan announced.

"Really? That's a first."

"I've had men here before," she said.

"Not in at least a year," Amber reminded her.

"Well, I've been busy." Between her dad's illness and trying to save her job, she hadn't had that much time to worry about dating and the few dates she'd been on had all been terrible. "I need to take this to Michael."

"Can I do it?" Hannah asked.

"Sure," she said, handing her niece the bottle. "My friend is sitting with Grandpa. Don't spill it."

"Okay, I won't," Hannah declared.

"So who is Michael?" Amber asked as she slid two trays of cookie sheets into the oven.

"He's a guy I went to school with. We ran into each other a few days ago at Playworld. He's competing for their PR account."

"So you're rivals again?" her mom said with a knowing smile. "Isn't that just crazy?"

"I certainly thought it was. I remember Dad mentioning that Michael had gotten hurt last season, but I guess I didn't realize the injury would end his career. Now he's working at his sister's firm and pitching for the same account I want."

"Just like old times," her mom said, adding for Amber's benefit, "Liz and Michael used to go head-to-head in school. He was a thorn in her side."

"More like a pain in the ass," she muttered.

Amber gave her a thoughtful look. "Then why bring him home to hang out with all of us?"

It was a good question. Fortunately, she had a logical answer. "I thought Dad might enjoy meeting him."

"And he did," her mom said. "His face lit up like a Christmas tree when you introduced Michael. I haven't seen Ron look that excited about anything in over a year. It was a good call, but what I want to know is what's really going on with you and Michael, Liz. He had his arm around you, and you looked quite friendly with the man I believe you once declared your sworn enemy."

"I was a little dramatic in high school."

Her mom laughed. "Not usually, but when it came to Michael, you definitely saw red. I can't count all the times you came home spitting mad from school, and his name was always on your lips."

"He pissed me off a lot."

"It sounds like you liked him," Amber interjected.

She shot her sister-in-law an annoyed look. "I did not like him."

"I think you did," her mother put in, agreeing with Amber. "That's why he bothered you so much."

"Because he was annoying and so good at everything. He wasn't just a great athlete, he was smart, too, and he always won whatever he went out for."

"He was quite popular," her mom agreed. "He was one of those kids that everyone liked, except you, of course."

"I have to meet this guy," Amber said with a laugh.

"Go for it," she told her sister-in-law. "I'll watch the cookies for you."

"Don't let the bottoms burn or Hannah will kill you," Amber said.

As Amber left the room, her mother gave her a gentle smile. "So, what's really going on, Liz?"

She sighed. "I have no idea. He's better than I remembered."

Her mom met her gaze. "Oh, honey, I always knew you had a big crush on him."

"Along with every other girl in school."

"Well, you're not in school anymore, and judging by the way he was looking at you a few minutes ago, I'd say he's definitely interested in you now."

"He's just trying to throw me off my game."

"You're always so suspicious. You get that from your dad. You don't let anyone in easily. And even when they're in your circle, you keep your eye on them. You're ready to bolt if someone is going to make a move to hurt you. I guess you have a very sharp survival instinct. But sometimes I worry that you'll push love away just because you're afraid of letting go, allowing the possibility of pain into your life. But, honey, sometimes you have to take a risk."

"I take risks."

"In your job, maybe. Although, I'm not even sure about that. It seems like you've gotten more cautious since your dad got sick."

"Well, I don't want to let him down. He has high expectations for me."

"I know. He wants you to be him." Her mom walked over and cupped her face with her hands. "But you're not him; you're you. And that's good, too."

For some reason, her mother's words brought unexpected moisture to her eyes. She blinked the tears away. "Thanks,

Mom."

"Any time. You've been a rock since your dad got sick. And I know you're doing everything you can to make him proud and to protect his interests. But I don't want you to lose yourself, Liz."

"I'm going to try not to," she said. But there was a small part of her that wondered if it might be too late to make that claim.

Chapter Seven

Liz had just taken the cookies out of the oven when Amber and Hannah came back into the kitchen.

"Oh, my God, Liz, Michael is gorgeous," Amber said. "You cannot throw this one back."

"He's not a fish. I didn't catch him."

"Maybe you did," Amber said with a grin. "He asked if you were coming back."

"Sounds like he needs a rescue."

"I don't know about a rescue, but I think he's missing you."

She sincerely doubted that. Michael was probably just feeling overwhelmed by the football in the family room. She put some of the freshly baked cookies onto a plate. "I'll take these out to the guys."

"And stay there," her mother said. "Amber and I have things under control and Kelly will be here soon."

"I was wondering where Kelly was," she said, referring to Greg's wife.

"She had to show a house today, but she'll be here soon."

"How's the real-estate going?"

"Better since the market picked up," her mom said. "Sometimes, I think your dad and I should sell this big house.

We really don't need all the rooms anymore."

She frowned at that. "You can't sell the house now. Not with Dad being sick and all."

"You're right. Now isn't a good time," her mom said, a more somber note in her eyes. "Forget I said it. Go entertain Michael."

After being pushed out of the kitchen, Liz made her way back into the family room. Her brothers and their boys were sprawled across all the chairs and couches, but Michael patted the small area of the couch next to him, so she slid in between him and her brother Tom.

"Where have you been?" Michael asked.

"Helping my mom in the kitchen. Everything okay out here?"

Before he could answer, her brothers jumped up, giving each other a high five as their team scored a touchdown."

"They're a little crazy," she told Michael.

"I've seen worse. It's actually kind of fun to be sitting with the fans. This is almost better than playing in the game."

"Almost?" she asked, raising a doubtful eyebrow.

"Okay, not even close, but it is fun. I haven't had an afternoon like this in a long time—make that ever."

"Really?" She wondered about the odd gleam in his eyes, but there was no opportunity to ask him to explain as her dad started peppering Michael with questions about the team's defensive line.

For the next few hours, there was nothing but football, family, and food. By seven o'clock, Liz had had enough of all three. After helping her mom clean up after dinner and seeing the guys ensconced in yet another game, she escaped up the stairs to her old bedroom.

The room was truly the room of her childhood. She'd moved out to go to college and except for a four-month-period right after college graduation; she hadn't lived in this house in a very long time. She smiled as she looked at the walls covered with her art. She'd certainly gone through some strange phases in her painting. At one time, she'd been obsessed with painting shadows of people. Other times, it was all about landscapes or crazy shapes.

And then there were the bookshelves filled with the books of her youth, adventures, mysteries, romance and biographies. She'd always been fascinated with the story of people's lives. Reading about how others made something special out of nothing had always inspired her to try a little harder.

"So this is where it all began," Michael said as he stepped into her room.

Her pulse jumped at his sudden presence and also at his words, because this was where it had all began—especially when it came to him. She'd spent quite a few hours lying on the bed, staring up at the ceiling thinking about him. Sometimes those thoughts had been filled with hate. Other times, there had been some lust involved... Her cheeks warmed at the thought.

"What?" he asked, his gaze narrowing.

"What do you mean?"

"You just thought of something that made your face red."

"It's warm in here."

"No, it's not."

"Well, it is to me."

"Okay," he said, putting up a hand. "We don't have to argue about everything."

His words made her realize that she'd always used an argument as a way to get past her feelings about him. She just hadn't understood it at the time.

"Look at your art," Michael said, waving his hand toward the walls. "You're really good, Liz."

"I was good. I haven't painted in a long time."

"You should start again."

"I don't have time."

"You can make time for things that are important." He paused. "You just go around once, Liz. You have to do what's in your heart."

"You sound like Charlie Hayward."

"I understand Charlie and his dream of creating a world where people can remember what it's like to believe in the impossible."

She sighed, his words reminding her that he was the competition, and he was probably going to give her a run for the money. But that was a problem for tomorrow. She didn't want to think about work right now.

Michael walked over to her desk and picked up a framed photograph taken at her college graduation. "Who are all these women?"

"My closest friends. That's Julie next to me. And then there's Laurel, Andrea, Kate, Isabella, Maggie and Jessica. We met freshmen year and we were best friends all through college. We're still pretty close. In fact, we made a vow at graduation that no matter how far apart we drifted, we'd always make sure to come back for each other's weddings."

"And who was it that just got married?"

"Laurel. She's the third from the left—the one who tossed me the bouquet."

He smiled at her grumpy tone. "I thought girls wanted to catch the bouquet."

"Well, I didn't. Now all I hear from them every time we get together is when am I going to find someone so I can make the bouquet toss come true."

"That's a lot of pressure." He set the photo down. "You're lucky, Lizzie. You have a wonderful family and a lot of good friends."

"I am lucky. I want you to know that I do appreciate how great you've been. You made this Sunday really nice for my dad, and he hasn't had a lot of good days lately."

"He's getting better though, right?"

She shrugged. "We don't really know. We hope so. But he has to get through this next round of chemo before they can tell us where he's at. This has been the worst thing I've ever had to go through. It's hard to see him sick, because he was always such a strong man. Now, sometimes I look at him, and he's so fragile. It's terrifying. He's not that old. He's in his early sixties. This shouldn't be happening now."

"You're right. He's too young."

She was glad that he didn't try to tell her everything would be all right, because no one knew that for sure, and the words always rang hollow. "Thanks." She walked over to the French doors leading out to a small deck. She needed a little air.

Michael followed her out on the deck. They stood in silence for a moment, looking out at the trees, the stars and the quiet night.

"This was my dreaming place," she murmured, not sure why she felt the need to tell him that, but ever since she'd come home, she'd lost some of her defenses.

"What did you dream about?"

"Becoming something amazing. I didn't know what that something would be, but I knew it was out there."

"Have you found it yet?"

She wanted to say yes, but the word wouldn't come out. She settled for, "I don't know."

"That means you haven't found it." He paused. "I saw you up here that night I came to your house to talk to you."

"The night you chickened out?"

"You were standing right here and there was a little glow over your head from the moonlight. You looked like an angel."

She stared at him in astonishment. "Are you serious?"

"I am," he said quietly, no trace of amusement in his eyes now. "You were beautiful then, Liz, and you're even prettier now. I really wanted to kiss you, and I wanted you to kiss me back, instead of punching me in the nose."

Her heart was suddenly thumping against her chest. "You had a girlfriend, I'm pretty sure."

"No, I didn't. There were girls around, but I wasn't seeing anyone in particular. No one interested me as much as you did."

"Maybe I was just a challenge," she suggested, her voice a little breathless, because she felt like one of her childhood dreams was coming true right this minute.

"You were always a challenge. You still are."

"You're trying to spook me, to manipulate me, to get my mind off our competition," she said, suddenly feeling a little desperate.

"No, Liz. I'm not thinking about work. I'm thinking about kissing you, right here, right now."

He moved forward and she backed up against the rail. She swallowed a lump in her throat. "So, what's stopping you?" she asked as his gaze moved from her eyes to her lips, but he made no move to make good on his desire.

"I don't think I could handle another broken nose."

She stared back at him, indecision running through her mind. But her mind was having a war right now with her body and with her emotions. It might be the stupidest move of her life, but she wanted to kiss Michael.

"I wouldn't hit you," she said softly.

"Is that a promise?"

She nodded. "Yes, but if you don't kiss me in the next ten seconds, I'm probably going to change—"

He cut off her words with a hot, purposeful kiss that went way beyond her wildest teenage imaginings. And Michael wasn't kissing her like a boy but like a man, a man who know what he wanted and expected to get it. Right now, he wanted her. She could hardly wrap her mind around that fact. But then her brain had turned to mush with the pressure of his lips against hers.

When he pulled her up against his chest, sliding his arms around her back, she went willingly. When his tongue slid along the seam of her lips in a restless determination to get inside, she opened her mouth, letting him take the kiss even deeper. And it still wasn't enough.

She wrapped her arms around his neck as he threatened to lift his head and take a breath. Not yet. She couldn't let him go. She needed another minute, another hour, another day or a year. And maybe that wouldn't be enough time.

His kisses had released a decade of pent-up emotions, and she had no idea how to stop the tidal wave that was running through her.

Finally, they broke apart, their breaths heating up the cool evening air.

Michael stared down at her with eyes that glittered in the moonlight. "What the hell," he muttered.

She didn't know what to say to that. Her brain was trying to kick itself back into gear.

"I didn't expect…" He stopped again. He couldn't seem to put together a full sentence, but she was no better. She couldn't even manage a few words.

He ran his hand down the side of her face. "Beautiful, Lizzie."

Her heart turned over at the tender side of his passion. Maybe he had liked her more than she'd ever believed. Or was she just caught up in her romantic fantasy coming to life? She had always been the practical girl, but the last thing she wanted to be right now was practical.

She drew in a breath, then another.

He smiled. "I didn't know that I could completely shut

you up with a kiss."

"It's comments like that that might get you punched in the nose again," she said lightly.

"There's the girl I remember."

"But I'm not that girl anymore, and you're not that guy, and this isn't high school. We got caught up in the moment, but the moment is over."

"It doesn't have to be. We're both single."

"We're competing against each other."

"That's business." He leaned forward, whispering in her ear. "This is personal."

She shivered as his warm breath hit her cheek. "We can't mix the two."

"It's too late."

"For tonight," she agreed, putting a hand on his chest to push him away. Only the feel of that solid chest made her really just want to curl her hands in the fabric of his shirt and pull him back to her. "Stop it."

"Stop what?" he asked, raising an eyebrow.

She frowned, realized she'd said the words out loud. "I was talking to myself."

"Really?" he asked with interest. "What did you want yourself to stop doing?"

"Everything. We need to leave now, Michael. We need to go back to Sacramento and regroup. Tomorrow we have to finish up at the park and then put together an initial pitch for Charlie by Thursday."

"I know. And we'll leave in a minute. We'll do everything you just said, but for now…" He shifted her so that she was facing outward. She leaned against his broad chest while his arms came around her waist. "Let's just enjoy the night for another minute. Then we'll go."

It was hard to fight something that felt so good, so she did what Michael asked. She let him hold her as she looked out at the stars and dreamed a new dream—one that couldn't possibly come true.

* * *

Liz fell asleep about twenty minutes into the drive back to Sacramento. Michael couldn't help thinking how she looked even prettier asleep. Her guard was completely down. There was no tension, no fight left in her body. She was completely relaxed and there even seemed to be a little smile on her slightly parted lips.

He shifted in his seat, turning his attention back to the road, but his mind wasn't on the highway or the traffic, it was on Liz, on what had happened on her balcony. He'd wanted to kiss her since he'd seen her fall into the quicksand outside of Charlie's office a few days earlier.

Actually, he'd wanted to kiss her since he'd tried to do that the last time—nine years ago.

She'd been worth the wait, he thought with a smile. And she hadn't hit him this time. No, she'd kissed him back with all her typical Lizzie fervor and passion. He liked her all worked up. In truth, back in school, sometimes he'd goaded her just to see that spark of fire in her eyes. She was definitely a woman who felt strongly about so many things.

One of those things was obviously her family.

His mind turned to her dad, to the man who had spent half the day talking football to him. Ron Palmer had been surprisingly astute when it came to football and it was clear he had a love for the game. But it was also clear that Ron had the same love for his family, a love they returned.

He hadn't been part of that kind of a family scene since his folks split up and probably not even before that. While he had good relationships with each member of his family, as a foursome they'd never been that tight. After being part of the

Palmer clan for a day, he felt like he'd missed something.

Actually, he knew he'd missed a lot, but he couldn't complain. Many people had had it a lot worse than him.

He glanced over at Liz as she mumbled something in her sleep. Her brows had drawn together, and it was clear her dreams were making her tense. Impulsively, he reached out and put his hand on her leg.

She let out a sigh and seemed to relax.

He smiled. The soothing touch might have driven away her tension, but it was creating a whole different kind of tension in his body.

He had it bad for her. He hadn't felt this turned on by a woman in a while. And while he knew she shared the attraction, he also knew that any relationship between the two of them was going to be complicated, maybe even impossible.

They were battling each other for a huge account. And after seeing Liz's affection for her ailing father, he knew she wanted the win for her dad as much as for herself.

But he couldn't just sit back and let that happen. He had his own family to consider. His sister needed a win, too. The Playworld account would ensure she had enough money to keep paying rent and wages to her employees. And Erica had bailed him out of a dark hole after his career ended. She'd given him something to get up for. He owed her.

Sighing, he put both hands back on the wheel. There was no great solution for the situation. One of them was going to win and one of them was going to lose.

Actually, it was possible neither one of them would win, but he didn't think so. He had celebrity contacts he could use and Liz had a strong firm behind her. Christa and Ed would have to put together something amazing to really be in the running.

It would almost be better if Christa or Ed won, then he wouldn't have to hurt Liz, and she wouldn't have to hurt him.

Somehow he didn't think that was the way it was going to go down.

Chapter Eight

Liz woke up in the hotel room Monday morning to the sound of her alarm. She scrambled to turn it off, then fell back against the pillows with a yawn. Yesterday had been a long day. She'd let her family and Michael distract her from work. She had to get her focus back today. She still had to visit a few more exhibits, talk to some employees and maybe even chat up a few tourists to get their impressions of the park. Then she had three rides to go on, including the monster roller coaster.

Her stomach clenched at the thought of getting on that ride. But she would do it. She had to do it. If she didn't go on the roller coaster, she would have no chance of winning the account. She could handle ninety seconds of terror and nausea, couldn't she?

Throwing back the covers, she jumped out of bed and hurried into the bathroom. After showering and changing into comfortable jeans and running shoes, she headed downstairs to grab breakfast in the lounge.

She wasn't the only one who'd had that idea. Sitting at a window table was Michael and Christa. They certainly seemed to be having a good time. Michael was talking and Christa was laughing. Then she put a hand on Michael's arm and leaned forward to whisper something in his ear.

Liz frowned at the flirtatious, intimate gesture. Just how friendly were Michael and Christa? She'd thought Michael was spending all of his time with her, but he'd obviously also found some time to schmooze it up with Christa.

Michael turned his head and caught her stare. He motioned her over. She reluctantly moved in their direction.

"Morning," he said, giving her a warm smile that felt far more intimate than it should have.

"Hi. Did you two already eat?" she asked.

"Just finished," Christa said. "I'm trying to convince Michael to shoot the moon with me."

"Well, don't let me stop you. I'm going to get some food. Maybe I'll see you around later."

"We can wait for you, Liz," Michael said.

"No, please go ahead. I have to make a few business calls before I go to the park."

Michael frowned at her answer, but Christa was already getting to her feet. "Let's go, Michael. I want to beat the crowds."

"I don't think there will be crowds on a Monday morning," he said.

"Even better. We can shoot the moon twice, maybe three times," Christa added with a sexy smile. "Trust me, you'll enjoy it a lot more when you're riding with me."

Liz shook her head at Christa's blatant innuendo. Christa reminded her a lot of the girls in high school who used to hang around Michael. Some things never changed.

She was relieved when they left the lounge. Despite the fact that from a business perspective, it might be dangerous to let Christa and Michael work together, she needed a little space from him so she could concentrate on her job, instead of thinking about how nice it would be to kiss him again. A yearning ache filled her gut at the memory. She tried to ignore it. She tried to pretend that Michael's kiss the night before had just reminded her that she'd been a little lonely the past year. It wasn't him that was so special. She'd just missed being with a man.

Sighing, she realized she'd never been a good liar, not even when it came to lying to herself.

Walking over to the buffet, she grabbed a bowl and filled it with oatmeal, then topped it off with blueberries and sat down at a table in front of the television. While she ate, she watched the morning news anchors talking about the upcoming holiday season. When the anchor threw to a field reporter, who was aptly named Autumn Dane, she sat up a little straighter.

"What incredible adventure have you found for us today, Autumn?" the anchor asked.

The beautiful red-haired Autumn waved her hand at the big barn behind her. "We've got pony rides for the kids, a holiday boutique for mom and a special beer tasting for dad. This is a great place for the whole family."

Autumn had certainly improved her news reporting skills since she and Liz had worked together as college interns at a television station. But she wasn't surprised that Autumn had done so well in her career. She'd always been determined and driven to get on TV.

As Autumn wrapped up her story, an idea ran through Liz's head. Autumn specialized in finding great places for the family to go and spend the weekend. What better place than Playworld?

Pulling out her phone, she was relieved to see she still had Autumn's number even though it had been a couple of years since they'd spoken. She sent her a quick text. "Just saw you on TV. You look great! I've got the perfect story idea for you. Call me when you get a chance. Even if you're not interested in the story, let's catch up."

She slipped her phone back in her bag, thinking how great

it would be if Autumn called her back before she had to make her pitch on Thursday. She'd love to be able to tell Charlie she'd already scheduled him for a national television spot.

Getting back into the swing of her job made her feel better, stronger and more in control. She was good at PR. She knew what to do. She just had to do it better than everyone else.

* * *

Michael didn't know what the hell was wrong with him. When had spending the morning with a beautiful woman become so boring? Christa was very attractive. He had to believe she was intelligent or she wouldn't be on this pitch, but he found her conversation dull and the over-the-top flirtation was more of a turnoff than anything else. He didn't want to cozy up with her in a dark ride as she suggested more than once. And when she'd squealed and clung to his arm while going over the rope bridge, he'd had to fight the urge to throw her off of it.

But it wasn't really her that was annoying him; it was Liz. It was the fact that he was stuck with Christa when he really wanted to be with Liz. But Liz had made it clear she wanted to be on her own. The warm, laughing, relaxed woman of the day before had definitely turned back into a cold, determined businesswoman this morning. She'd wanted him to see she had her game face back on. And he'd seen it all right. He just hadn't liked it.

"Michael, are you listening?" Christa asked.

"Sorry, what did you say?"

She tipped her head toward the man by the drinking fountain. Ed Hoffman was perusing the Playworld map through thick reading glasses. Dressed in black slacks and a white button-down shirt, he looked quite out of place in the park.

"There's no way Ed wins this," Christa said, echoing Michael's earlier thoughts. "He's too stiff and straight. Charlie wants someone who knows how to have fun, and from what I've seen that makes you and me the leaders. Because Liz Palmer is definitely low on the fun scale."

"Liz knows how to have fun," he said, not sure why he felt the need to defend her, but he did.

"If you say so," Christa said doubtfully. "She sure doesn't show it."

"She's serious when she's working."

"Are you sure there's nothing between you two?"

Nothing like a smoldering kiss on Liz's balcony and nine years of thinking about her? "We're just old friends," he said. He had no intention of sharing his feelings about Liz with Christa.

As if on cue, Liz came around the corner with a huge pink cone of cotton candy in her hand. And on her face was the biggest smile—a smile that quickly turned into a frown when she saw them.

"Hey," she said.

"How's the cotton candy?"

"Really good," she admitted, a guilty gleam in her eyes. "I haven't eaten this stuff since I was probably ten years old, but it tastes even better than I remember."

"Because it's pure sugar," Christa told her. "You're lucky you don't worry about your weight."

Liz's gaze narrowed as if she were debating whether or not Christa had just insulted her. Michael quickly stepped into the breach.

"Sugar is what makes it good," he said, trying to think of a way to ditch Christa and go around the park with Liz. "Where did you get it?"

"There was a stand by the pirate's cove."

"I'll have to check that out." As he finished speaking, Ed

saw them and ambled over.

"Hello," Ed said. "How are you all doing?"

"Great," Michael replied. "Are you enjoying the park?"

"Yes. It's well organized, clean and functional. The line control is excellent. Entertainment along the lines makes the wait feel shorter, which will be more important in the summer. The employees have excellent training and except for a few odd sorts, they have been generally quite polite and courteous."

"Sounds like you're having a hell of a good time," Christa quipped, sending Michael a pointed look.

Yeah, Ed was not going to win this account. His clinical approach to the park would not sit well with Charlie, not that all the things Ed had described weren't important, but they weren't things Michael had been considering at all. Maybe it was a good idea he'd crossed paths with Ed. He couldn't forget that there was a business side to the park that needed to be considered in promotional plans.

"That sounds a little dull, Ed," Christa added. "Charlie Hayward wants fun."

"Mr. Hayward wants to make money," Ed returned. "And I'm going to help him do that."

"You haven't won yet," Christa muttered.

"Neither have any of you."

Michael looked over at Liz, silently sending her a pleading smile to take him away from the others.

She gave him an indecisive look, then finally said, "I can show you where to get the cotton candy if you want, Michael."

"I do," he said eagerly.

"Really, Michael?" Christa asked with dismay. "I thought we were going to ride the whirlwind next."

"Why don't you and Ed do it together?"

Christa did not look happy about that idea, but surprisingly Ed jumped on it. "I would like to get a woman's perspective," he said. "And in return, I'll give you a man's perspective. It think it will be quite helpful to you."

"Awesome," Christa replied, her tone not at all supporting her words.

"We'll catch up with you later," Michael said quickly.

"Let's make sure to do that," Christa said, sending him a pointed look.

"Do you really want cotton candy?" Liz asked when Christa and Ed disappeared around the corner.

"How about a bite of yours?"

She held out the cone and he swirled a cloud of pink onto his fingers and then popped it into his mouth. "It's like eating sweet air," he said.

Liz laughed. "That's a good way to put it. You're really good with words. I'm going to have to keep that in mind."

"Thanks for bailing me out."

"You weren't having fun with Christa hanging on to your arm?"

"Like an incredibly heavy anchor? No. She might be a good PR specialist, but she's irritating as hell."

"She's very attractive."

"Until she opens her mouth."

"You used to hang out with girls like Christa in high school. In fact, when I saw you this morning, I felt like I had stepped back in time. If Christa had been wearing cheerleading skirt, it would have felt exactly the same as it did before."

"Cheerleaders tend to hang around football players."

"Oh, I know that. It's the perk of every quarterback, isn't it?"

"It *was* a perk," he admitted. "But I'm past looking to hang out with groupies. That was part of another life."

"No groupies in the PR world, but there are other perks."

"Like?"

"Like going to an amusement park and eating cotton candy on a Monday."

He smiled. "Thank God you're back."

His words wiped the grin off her face and brought a puzzled look to her brown eyes. "What do you mean?"

"This morning you were all business, not at all like the woman I spent yesterday with. The woman who showed me what I missed all those years ago."

Her cheeks turned pink at his words, and her eyes glittered in the morning sunshine. "We got off track last night."

"I was hoping to get further off track, but when we got back to the hotel, you ran into your room pretty fast."

"I didn't want us to make an even bigger mistake."

"Kissing you wasn't a mistake."

"It was considering the circumstances. We're together because of a job, so let's focus on that."

He knew she was right. This wasn't the right time or the right place to explore a relationship with Liz, but when he wanted something, he didn't like to wait. And he wanted Liz.

"What are you thinking?" she asked warily.

"Trust me, you don't want to know."

"Okay. Do you want the rest of this?"

"Sure." He took the cotton candy off her hands. "What do you think of Ed's take on the park?"

"I think he's going to be easy to beat."

"Me, too."

"So, it's really a race between you, me and Christa. She does have a lot of energy and a way with men, which is always an advantage."

"I'm positive that Christa will use any advantage she can find," he said, finishing off the cotton candy. He tossed the cardboard spool into a nearby recycle bin. "And I do think she may have an advantage over you."

His words made her stiffen, and she gave him a sharp look. "What's her advantage? That she dresses more provocatively, that she's a better flirt? What?"

"She's not afraid of roller coasters and you are." He saw the truth in her eyes. "You haven't been on the big one yet, and there's no way you win this pitch if you can't shoot the moon."

"I'm going to get on the ride," she said, trying to sound convincing.

"Prove it. Let's do it now. We'll go together."

"I don't need a babysitter, Michael."

"How about a friend?"

She stared back at him, confusion in her gaze. "I never really thought you and I could be friends."

"But we are, aren't we?"

"Honestly, Michael, I don't know what we are, but I can't worry about it right now."

"Agreed. What's important now is to get you on the roller coaster. Get the elephant off your back, Liz. You'll feel a lot better."

"All right, let's go," she said. "It's not that big of a deal. It's ninety seconds. I can do anything for ninety seconds."

"Of course you can," he said as they made their way across the park. "It will be over before you know it."

As they walked across the park, he could feel Liz's tension increasing. She was walking like someone about to be executed. Every step was a little slower, slightly more hesitant. But he kept pushing her along, a gentle nudge in her back when she started to falter. Finally, they reached the end of the line. He was happy to see it wouldn't be more than a ten minute wait. Any longer, and Liz would probably bolt. Hopefully, she could make it the ten minutes.

She looked up at the monstrous structure rising above them. "Who ever thought these things were a good idea?"

"People who like danger," he said.

"You do know that there's a good chance I'm going to throw up that cotton candy all over you."

"I'll risk it."

"You are a brave man," she said dryly. "But I'm not kidding. I've never been good on rides. My brain can't seem to make sense of what's happening, which end is up, and that sends my stomach into a nauseous spin."

"I'm sorry you have to go through this."

"You know that by forcing me to get on this, I'm one step closer to beating you."

"Well, if I'm going to win, I want it to be on merit, and not because of a forfeit. If you don't go on this ride, you automatically lose." He paused. "Although there's a good chance you'll lose anyway and then this will be for nothing. So it's really up to you."

"I don't intend to lose."

"Well, one of us will lose," he couldn't help pointing out.

"It's not going to be me. I have to bring this account home."

He understood her motivation a little better now that he'd spent time with her family. "You know your father is already really proud of you. He told me that yesterday. He said he admires you more each day."

"That was really sweet of him to say." She wiped her eye with her fingers.

"Sorry, I didn't mean to make you feel bad."

"I seem to be overflowing with emotions lately." She cleared her throat. "My dad liked you. So did everyone else in my family. Amber said you were a good listener, and she was right. You didn't try to take over the conversation."

"That would have been difficult to do even if I wanted to. Your brothers talk a lot."

She smiled. "They do. So do most of the men I go out with. I can rarely get a word in about myself before they change the topic back to whatever interests them."

"You've obviously been dating the wrong men."

"I can't argue with that," she said with a little laugh. "I'm not good at dating. There's so much game playing, so many rules. You can't text him back for twenty-four hours or he'll think you're too clingy. Or you have to do drinks not dinner because dinner is too much like a date. It's hard to remember it all."

"So, don't. Just be yourself."

"That's not what my girlfriends say."

"Maybe they're not giving you the best advice. I'm offering you a man's perspective."

"A man who doesn't have long-term serious relationships."

He tipped his head. "Point taken. But I still think it's better to be yourself. Otherwise, who are they getting to know? It will blow up at some point."

"You might be right about that." She drew in a deep breath as they neared the front of the line. "I don't know if I can do this."

He grabbed her hand and squeezed his fingers around hers. "You can do it, Liz. There's nothing you can't do."

"I want to believe that."

"Believe it. If there's anyone in this world who has had the opportunity to be amazed by you, it's me."

Her gaze narrowed. "Really? When were you amazed by me?"

"Every time we competed."

"But you always won."

"Sometimes I got lucky. Sometimes I played the popularity card, I'll admit that. But you—you were always so prepared, so determined and strong. You made me better because you played against me." As he said the words, he realized how true they were. He'd missed Liz after high school. Luckily, he'd had other players to compete against in football, but in the rest of his life, there had been a void.

"You made me better, too," she admitted. "But if you repeat that to anyone, I will deny it."

"Understood."

The cars pulled up in front of them, and they had the fortune—or misfortune—to get the first row.

He let go of Liz's hand while they buckled in and the bar came down over their laps. Then he put his hand on her leg as the ride began to roll. She had a death grip on the bar in front of them, and he could feel the tension in her body.

"Try to embrace it," he advised. "Don't fight it. Go with it. Let yourself fly."

"What I don't want to do is fly over this bar," she yelled back at him.

"You're safe. That's why people love roller coasters. They scare the crap out of you, but you're not going to die."

"Oh, God," she groaned as they began their steep ascent. "I really hope you're right about the not dying part."

"Here we go," he said as they crested the first peak. "Hang on, Lizzie."

"Trust me, I am not going to let go."

Her words ended in a scream as they went flying down the track.

Chapter Nine

She was going to die.

Liz clung to the bar as the car swerved around a sharp curve, then down a stomach-dropping fall and up and over another track heading straight for the loop that would turn them completely upside down. It was there before she knew it. One minute she was looking at the sky, and the next, she was heading straight toward the ground. Then she was jerked up again. Her body seemed to be flying around the seat. She prayed that she would stay inside the car as the wind stung her face as they spun around another screaming curve. One more sharp fall, another hairpin turn, and then the coaster came to a crashing stop.

Her chest heaved with terror-filled breaths, her stomach churning, her eyes darting every which way as she tried to focus, tried to tell herself she was safe. The ride was over.

"You made it, Liz," Michael said, putting his hand over hers. "You did it."

"Are you sure we're not dead?"

"Positive." He laughed and jumped out of the car, extending his hand to help her out.

She gladly took his hand, not at all sure she could actually get out of the car on her own. She was still shaking as they walked toward the exit, and she found herself hanging onto

Michael's hand and clinging to his side. They left the ride area and headed toward a bench a dozen yards away.

She sat down hard, her head still spinning. She didn't know where to look; the world was moving in front of her.

"Liz," he said sharply, squatting in front of her, his hands on her knees now. "Focus. Look at me."

She followed his order. "I'm trying, but there are three of you right now."

"Just keep your gaze on one point."

She drew in a couple more deep breaths, relieved when her vision started to improve. "There's only one of you now," she muttered.

"Happy to hear it. Can I get you some water?"

"I just need to breathe for a minute."

"Okay." He gave her a worried look. "Are you going to be sick?"

"I'm hoping not." She wished she could be more confident, but her stomach was threatening to make that a lie.

"Keep breathing. Let things settle down."

His calm voice was surprisingly helpful. A few minutes later, she started to feel like she might be out of the throw-up zone. "It's better," she said. She put hands over his and gave him a weak smile. "Thanks."

"You're welcome." Relief filled his gaze. "You're going to be all right. Especially when you start to realize that it's over. You're done with the last hurdle here at Playworld."

That did help speed her recovery. "I like the sound of that."

"Did you have any fun at all?"

"Are you crazy?" she asked in amazement. "Who could have fun on that?"

He laughed. "Millions of people. It's the most popular ride in the park."

"It was horrible. I never ever want to do that again."

"I wouldn't put that quote in your PR pitch."

She made a face at him. "Believe me, I won't. And I hope my reaction stays between the two of us."

"Of course." He stood up and sat down on the bench next to her. "But it still may be hard for you to sell something you don't love."

"I know all the right buzzwords to use. And I don't have to love something to be able to sell it."

"Charlie wants you to love it. That's the whole point of our time here at the park."

"I love the rest of the park, so I'm going to be fine." She paused. "Thanks for being supportive, Michael. I do appreciate it. I'm not sure I would have actually gotten on that ride if you hadn't forced me to do it."

"I think you would have made it. You don't quit, even when you're scared. I'm going to get us some waters."

"I'd like that."

As Michael walked away, she settled back against the bench, breathing in and out for a few more moments. While she still felt a little sick, she also felt proud of herself for doing what she needed to do. As Michael had said, she wasn't a quitter. She always fought to the end, even if she was losing. She just didn't know any other way to play.

Her phone buzzed, and she pulled it out of her purse, seeing her friend Andrea's face pop up on the screen wanting to do a video call. "Hey Andrea."

"Hi Liz, where are you?" Andrea asked.

"I'm recovering from my roller coaster ride at Playworld."

"Did you throw up?" Andrea asked.

"No, thank goodness. What are you doing?"

"I'm meeting with Kate." Andrea shifted and Kate Marlowe's pretty face popped up behind her.

"We're having an early lunch," Andrea said.

"And that's not all," Kate added.

Liz could see the excitement on both of their faces. "What is going on?"

Andrea held up her left hand and showed off a gorgeous square diamond ring.

"Oh my God," Liz said in shock. "Is that an engagement ring?"

"Yes, Alex proposed to me last night," Andrea replied.

"It's gorgeous. But, wow, this is fast. It's only been a few months."

"Super fast," Andrea agreed. "But Alex and I are in love, and we want to get married. There just doesn't seem any reason to wait. I know he's the one. And he feels the same way about me."

"Well, that's great. I'm so happy for you. I'm a little shocked, but this is really wonderful."

"I know you're supposed to be the next bride," Andrea said. "But—"

"Please, don't even think about that," she said with a laugh. "Do you have a date already?"

"We're thinking around Valentine's Day, if Kate can make the magic happen that fast."

"It will be a challenge," Kate said. "But I am good at my job."

"And of course you'll be a bridesmaid, Liz. Laurel will be my maid of honor, but I want the whole gang back for my wedding."

"You know we'll be there for you," she promised. Liz looked up as Michael handed her a bottle of water. "Thanks," she said.

"Who's that?" Kate asked curiously.

She realized she'd turned her phone giving her friends a good view of Michael. "This is Michael Stafford," she said. "My good friends, Andrea and Kate."

"You're the guy from high school?" Andrea asked.

"That's me," Michael said, smiling at her friends.

"Is it really true that you beat Liz at everything?" Kate asked.

He laughed. "I see my reputation has preceded me."

She'd forgotten that she'd told them about Michael at Andrea's birthday party on Friday. "We have to go. You can talk to Michael another time."

"Maybe next weekend," Kate said. "We're going to have an engagement party on Sunday— location to be determined."

"Let me know, and I'll be there," she said, ending the call.

"Which one is getting married?" Michael asked.

"Andrea."

"Blonde or brunette?"

"Blonde. Andrea is a journalist for *World News Today*." Liz took a sip of her bottled water, her head spinning once again and this time it wasn't from the roller coaster. "She interviewed the billionaire game maker Alex Donovan two months ago for the magazine cover story, and along the way they fell in love. Now they're engaged."

"Fast work. And she found herself a billionaire."

"She did, but Andrea isn't about the money. She's one of those reporters who just have to tell the truth, expose injustice in the world. I think that's what Alex liked about her. She's down to earth and she really cares about people. I'm super happy for her."

"Looks like you're going to have a chance to catch another bouquet."

She groaned. "I am definitely going to pick a better place to stand this time. Thanks for the water. I'm feeling a lot better."

"Good."

She looked around them, taking a few moments to just soak in the happy atmosphere of the park. Every person within her gaze seemed to be having a good time. "I wonder how Ed and Christa are doing," she mused.

"I'm sure they've ditched each other by now."

"Probably. So I think I'm done with the park. It's time to go home and start coming up with some brilliant ideas for Thursday's meeting."

"Do you know your angle yet?"

"I have some ideas, but I need to let it all sink in, or at least let get my stomach back from the roller coaster."

"So you might take a break tonight, not jump right into work?"

She tilted her head, giving him a curious look. "Why do you ask?"

"I have an idea."

"Am I going to like it?"

"I'm not sure *I* like it."

His words puzzled her. "What are you talking about, Michael?"

"I told you that my old coach wants me to meet him before the game tonight. I was thinking you could go with me. Have you ever been to a pro game?"

"No, never. My dad used to have tickets with my grandfather, but my brothers were usually first in line to go."

"I can get you down on the field."

She thought about his invitation and saw the strain in his eyes. "You don't really want to go, do you?"

"It sounds strange to say no. My whole life, all I wanted to do was play on a pro team. Now, I don't even know if I want to go to a game."

"Then why are you going?"

"Because Hank keeps calling me."

"That's not the reason."

He tipped his head. "Because I can't stop thinking about his offer and whether I made the right decision to cut football out of my life." He paused. "I have to say that yesterday kind of broke the ice for me. Watching games with your family forced me back into it. And your dad asked me so many questions, I never really had time to think about the fact that I wasn't playing anymore."

"You were a good sport," she said.

"So is it your turn to be a good sport?" he asked hopefully. "I could use a friend."

"Everyone on that team is your friend."

"They'll be playing. I need someone standing by my side."

She blew out a breath, knowing that she should spend the night working on her pitch. On the other hand, she owed Michael. He'd not only made her dad's weekend, he'd also helped her take on the roller coaster.

"All right. I'll go," she said. "As long as we can get those garlic fries. I love those."

"Cotton candy and garlic fries, my kind of woman."

"Well, I wouldn't eat them at the same time," she protested.

He laughed. "I might. And maybe add in a beer chaser."

"Now, you've gone too far," she teased.

"Let's go back to the hotel and check out."

She stood up, relieved that her legs didn't feel like rubber anymore. "I think I can actually walk again. I don't really remember how I got from the roller coaster to here."

"I practically carried you."

"Really? I thought I was still flying."

He smiled. "You're a gamer, Liz."

"Just what every girl wants to hear."

"It's a compliment. And if I told you how I really see you, you wouldn't believe me anyway."

She wasn't sure what to make of that comment. "I'm not going to ask."

"Well, maybe someday I'll tell you anyway—when you're ready to hear me."

Chapter Ten

Liz was still thinking about Michael's cryptic words when she drove back to San Francisco. After checking out of the hotel, they'd each gotten in their cars and were currently tailgating their way back to the bay. Michael had let her lead, and she couldn't help thinking how happy she felt every time she looked in the rearview mirror and saw him. It felt good to have him so close.

Actually, being with Michael just felt good in general. It was a dangerous, heady, somewhat out of control feeling, kind of like riding that roller coaster, only a lot better. She tried to remind herself that once the competition was over, Michael would be out of her life, but that didn't change the way she felt right now. For once, she was going to let the future take care of itself and live in the moment.

She hit a fair amount of traffic going into the city and it was almost four by the time she reached her apartment building in North Beach. She pulled into the underground parking lot, hoping Michael could find a nearby spot. She wanted to drop off her bag and grab a jacket before going to the stadium.

When she got into the lobby from the garage, she saw Michael waiting outside the front door with his suitcase. He didn't want to leave it in his truck while they were at the game, but having his suitcase in her apartment meant he was going to have to come up after the game to get it. She'd worry about that later.

"This is a nice neighborhood," Michael said as she let him in.

"I love the area. I have a couple of friends who live nearby and there are great restaurants, bars and it's short walk to the pier."

"Sounds perfect," he said, following her up the stairs to her second floor apartment.

"Don't expect much," she warned as she opened the door and ushered him inside. "It's just a big studio."

"But you have a lot of room," he commented, glancing around.

She did have some space. The large room was divided into three areas, one for sleeping, one for sitting and one for cooking. Her double bed was hidden behind an ornamental screen. She had a couch and an armchair by the window, and her kitchenette offered seating at a counter with two stools. A small bathroom was just behind the kitchen and walk-in closet. She was happy she'd done her laundry a few days earlier. And since she hadn't been home much the past few days, the place was pretty neat.

"I like the light," he said. "But where's your art? Your walls are pretty bare."

"It's back at my parents' house."

"You really don't feel the urge to paint anymore?"

"I've done some sketches, but nothing good enough to hang on a wall."

"I doubt that."

"Well, I just haven't gotten around to decorating. I've been busy. Maybe I should see your place, because I have a feeling it's not going to look like it came out of the pages of a design magazine." She paused, frowning. "Actually, I'm probably wrong. It would make sense if you had your home professionally decorated. You must have made a lot of money in football. Where do you live exactly?"

"I have a small house in the Berkeley hills. My sister's friend Carmen helped me decorate it. She's not a professional, and I paid her in tickets for last year's playoff game. You'll have to come over and check it out."

"Why Berkeley? Why not San Francisco?"

"I enjoy having a little more space than I'd have here in the city. Plus, I have a great view of the bay from my deck. I've seen some amazing sunsets. As an artist, you'd love the colors."

She would love the colors. His words had already created an image in her mind. It was funny that Michael was making her think about painting again. He hadn't just taken her back in time to high school, but to a place in her life where she'd been filled with a lot of passion for art. She still had passion; she was just more practical now. She was an adult. Being practical came with age, didn't it?

Shaking her head, she walked across the room, grabbed a jacket out of her closet and said, "Let's go to the game."

After leaving her apartment, they got into Michael's truck and drove south of the city to a beautiful new football stadium that had been built three years earlier. It sat on land right next to the bay and as they got out of the truck, a gust of wind lifted Liz's hair off of her neck and she quickly zipped up her jacket.

They'd gotten a spot in preferred parking, but as they walked toward the stadium entrance, Liz could see dozens of cars already in the main lot. Small barbecues were smoking with delicious smells of barbecue.

"People come really early," she said. "The game doesn't start for another hour and a half."

"Sometimes they come in the morning. It's part of the

experience."

"I think I prefer the experience of sitting in my parents' family room with my mom making a lot of great food."

"That was good, I must admit."

As they neared the private entrance designated for players and coaches, Michael's body tensed. He blew out a breath. "I don't know if I'm ready for this," he muttered.

She had a feeling he was talking more to himself than to her, but she couldn't help responding. "You're going to be fine, Michael. As you told me earlier—right before the roller coaster took off—you're not going to die."

"That was quite a pep talk I gave you, wasn't it?" he said dryly.

"You were right." She paused. "I don't know what you're going through, how difficult this might be for you, but I do know that, like me, you never back down from a challenge."

"I just don't know what I'm doing here, Liz. I'm done with football."

"Then this should be easy. Say hello and goodbye and you'll have closure."

"I thought I had closed this chapter in my life. It's Hank who's trying to open it all up again."

"You're not going to be able to move forward until you deal with this offer. You said that yourself earlier. That's why we're here, so there's no backing out now."

He let out a frustrated sigh. "Why do you have to be so smart, Lizzie?"

"Apparently, so I can annoy you."

He smiled. "You do get under my skin."

"Likewise. But you brought me here for a reason and I think that reason had something to do with making sure you walked through the door."

"I had other reasons, too."

"Well, let's stick with that one for now." She opened the

door and waved him through it.

After giving their name to the security guard, they were handed credentials and tickets for a sky box and then cleared to walk through the tunnel to the field. Liz had been in stadiums before, but never on the field of a professional football game. Despite how early they were, there was quite a crowd of people on the field and also in the stands. Music blared and videos of past highlight plays were featured on the big screens around the stadium. The atmosphere was filled with energy and excitement. She could see the anticipation on the faces of the players who were running through their warm-up drills.

They paused at the edge of the track.

"So this was you a year ago," she said, thinking that this was her first real glimpse into Michael's old life.

He nodded, his jaw so stiff she thought it might break. "I always loved game day. I couldn't wait to get out here. And if it was a night game like this, I had even more hours to get amped up for the battle ahead."

"My dad said you were a great quarterback."

"I wasn't bad," he admitted.

"Humble? That isn't usually the Michael Stafford style."

His grim expression eased as he looked at her. "Okay, you're right. I was good and I could have been great if I'd had more years to play. But that wasn't in the cards."

"The players are bigger in person. How did you handle getting hit by some 300 pound linebacker?"

"Most of the time, I was able to escape. I had a good offensive line. They protected me."

"What happened the day you got hurt?"

"It was a very close game. We were down to the last minute. I was scrambling. I got hit hard, but it wasn't the first hit that took me out, it was the second one by an overly aggressive player. I fell badly and my knee was torn up."

"Isn't that called roughing the quarterback?"

"Yeah, it was a penalty. The team took yardage for the play, but that wasn't much consolation when I was headed to the hospital."

"Have you ever talked to the guy who hit you?" she asked curiously. "Did you know him?"

"I did know him. He came to see me after my surgery. He wanted to apologize. He said he was caught up in the moment."

She could see shadows of emotion in his eyes, but she couldn't quite read what those emotions were. "How did you react? Were you angry? Did you let him have it?"

"No, I told him I understood what it meant to get caught up in the game."

"That was generous. You let him off the hook for an illegal play that ended your career."

Michael frowned. "He wasn't trying to hurt me. He just wanted to win."

"The end justifies the means?" she queried.

"You're twisting my words, Lizzie."

"I don't think I am. Winning at any cost isn't really winning, not when cheating is involved."

"It's not that simple." Michael paused as a man in a red windbreaker made his way over to them.

The older man had to be Hank, Liz thought. He had gray hair and a wrinkled face weathered by sun, but he moved with the agility of someone who had once been an athlete himself.

Hank threw his arms around Michael, giving him a bear hug. Then he stepped back, a pleased smile on his face. "Thanks for coming."

"You didn't give me much choice. You've been putting the heat on hard."

"Had to. Season is halfway done. We need to change things around now. I want you to take a look at the offense with me. You know these guys. You played with them. And you know the strengths and weaknesses of our rookie quarterback. I want you to give me your thoughts. And then we'll talk about how we can make you a permanent part of the team."

"I'll watch some of the game," Michael said. "That's as far as my commitment goes."

"You'll stay as long as you need to," Hank said somewhat cryptically. His gaze moved to Liz. "Want to introduce me, Michael?"

"Liz Palmer, Hank Grandietti, one of the best coaches in the business."

"Pleasure," Hank said, shaking her hand. "Michael was one of the best players I ever had the privilege to coach. Did you ever see him play?"

"I saw him play in high school."

"So you two go way back?" Hank said, curiosity in his eyes.

"We do," she said.

"I've got you set up in a sky box," Hank added. "But you're welcome to stay on the field."

"I think I'm going to go find something to eat," Liz said. "And then I'll go to the box. Take your time, Michael. If you need to stay on the field, stay on the field, I'll be fine."

"I'll be up before the game starts."

"Whatever works. Just point me in the right direction."

Hank waved his hand toward the entrance. As she left she heard Hank jump into what problems they were having with their offense. She had a feeling this game was going to make it much more difficult for Michael to shut the door on football, no matter how much he wanted to do that. Well, she'd gotten him through the door. The rest was up to him.

* * *

Michael's gaze followed Liz across the field.

"Girlfriend?" Hank asked, pausing for a moment from his football talk.

"Not really sure what we are," he said, turning back to Hank. "But she's important."

Hank grinned. "Don't screw it up then."

"Always great to get your advice."

"Your turn for advice. Come with me."

Michael followed Hank onto the field, exchanging greetings and hugs with the men who had been his friends and teammates the last couple of years. He realized how long it had been since he'd seen some of them. And that was mostly his fault. He'd ignored the calls, texts and emails after his surgery and long rehab. A few of the guys he had eventually called back, but by then there didn't seem to be much to say. He didn't want to talk about football, and he wasn't sure what else there was to talk about.

But now he realized that along with football, he'd shut a lot of people out of his life just because they were associated with the game he couldn't play anymore. Fortunately, no one seemed to hold that against him.

As the players ran through their warm-up drills, he felt a deep, aching yearning in his soul for the game that had driven his life since he was six years old.

This was why he hadn't wanted to see anyone, hadn't wanted to go to a game. It had been a little easier at Liz's house. Then the game had been on TV, and he could look at it like a show, but here on the sidelines, all the sounds, smells and sights were very familiar.

"Jim has a good arm, we all know that," Hank said, referring to the young quarterback. "But he's jittery when he gets out of the pocket. He doesn't move like you did and the rest of the team senses his nerves. Some of them are overplaying to compensate. It's not working."

He watched Jim throw, his experienced eyes noting the little details, the balance, the arm strength and the situational awareness. Everything looked good, but these were just drills. The actual game would challenge all of Jim's skills.

For the next forty minutes, he and Hank talked their way through the offensive line and the list of plays. Michael made a few suggestions. He couldn't help himself. He hadn't come here to get involved, but it was hard to walk away from his training and his desire to help the team. Before he knew it, they were two minutes away from kickoff.

"Let's talk after the game," Hank said, slapping him on the back.

"Tomorrow," he replied. "I'll put together some thoughts for you."

"Good," Hank said.

"But you know what you're doing out there, Hank. You're one of the best. You don't need me. You're just second-guessing yourself."

"I don't think so. You were the captain of these guys. You know them better than anyone. You had a gift for bringing out the best in them. And I really want you to consider making your involvement a more permanent thing. Just think about it. You can't play anymore, but you can make a difference in the game that you love."

Michael didn't reply, mostly because he didn't have an answer. He'd really thought he'd turned the corner...until now.

Chapter Eleven

Liz was sitting alone in the front row of the luxurious box. She was eating her way through a pile of garlic fries, and there was a tall beer in front of her. She turned her head and gave him a smile. "Hey, did you know we get free food in here?"

He laughed as he sat down beside her. "I've never actually been up here."

"A waitress comes by like every five minutes. Want a fry? They're very garlicky, so you should join me or sit in the next row."

He smiled and took a fry, popping it into his mouth. "Delicious."

"Aren't they? I love these things. So bad for me, but there you go." She gave him a searching look as he took another fry. "How did it go down there?"

"Fine. I'll take some notes for Hank and talk to him tomorrow."

"What about the job?"

"I told him I have a job already."

"I know, but is it the job you really want? You've been all over me about giving up my painting. Aren't you doing the same thing?"

"You had a choice to keep painting; I didn't."

"It sounds like you have a choice now," she said.

He let out a sigh. "I don't know. I feel like I'd be ripping a bandage off a wound that wasn't healed yet."

"I get it," she said with an understanding nod. "Football was your life. It was your connection to your dad. It was more than a game; it was everything. And then fate dealt you a really bad hand. But to your credit, you got back up, took action and made changes.

"Exactly."

"And that's all great. But something new has opened up for you now, an option you hadn't considered before. And I think you were smart to come here and consider it. In fact, I think it was pretty brave."

He was surprised at the admiration in her gaze. It was not the kind of look he usually got from her. "Well, thanks."

"You're welcome. And since you haven't said I'm wrong about anything; I must be right."

"You always like to be right."

"I usually am," she said.

Her playful smile drew him in. He didn't think about what he wanted to do. He just did it. He leaned over and kissed her surprised mouth and then gave her a grin. "Thanks. And, wow, that is a lot of garlic."

She laughed. "I thought it might ward you off."

"A little garlic doesn't scare me away." He paused. "And for the record, you were right about pretty much everything. Now, I'm going to go find that waitress. I feel like something a little heartier than fries."

"I was thinking about the French Dip," she said.

"You got it. Anything else?"

"No, I'm good."

As he left the box, he felt surprisingly good, too, and that was all because of Liz. She had a way of looking at things that cut through all the bullshit—at least when it came to him.

When it came to her own life, he thought she might need to take some of her own advice. But it was easier to see in others what you couldn't see in yourself. Bottom line—he was just exceptionally happy that they'd run into each other again. And for tonight, he was going to stop worrying so much about the decisions facing him and just have some fun with a beautiful, competitive, smart-mouthed woman who made his pulse race every time she looked in his direction.

* * *

Liz had more fun with Michael than she'd expected to have. She didn't know why no one else came to the box during the game, but she enjoyed the private oasis of luxury. During the game, Michael shared some of his thoughts about the offense. It didn't take long for her to realize why Hank had asked for Michael's input. Michael had tremendous insight into the minds of the players. He knew their strengths and weaknesses, knew which physical movements came naturally to them, what their instincts were when they were in trouble, how they reacted to pressure. He was really an amazing analyst, and by the fourth quarter she was wondering just how he could *not* take the job Hank was offering.

A Blackhawks rep from the team came into the box just before the game ended and handed Michael a signed jersey and football.

"What's this?" Liz asked.

"I asked my friend Keith Saxton if he could sign these for your dad."

She was stunned when he handed her the signed jersey with a message that read: *Stay strong, Ron. We're rooting for you. Keith Saxton.* Her eyes blurred with moisture as she gazed back at Michael. "You did this for my dad?"

"I know he's a big fan. It's not a big deal."

"It is a really big deal." She was incredibly touched by his thoughtfulness and generosity. He'd been caught up in his own inner turmoil, but still he'd taken the time to think of her dad. She set down the jersey and then threw her arms around Michael's neck. She gave him a hug and a kiss. "Thank you."

"You're welcome," he said, sliding his arms around her waist. He gave her a mischievous grin. "I did get your dad two things, so maybe another kiss…"

She smiled and pressed her lips against his once again.

He tasted like beer, garlic and Michael. It was a dizzying combination, and the kiss went off far longer than it should have. Finally, they broke apart.

She could hear the crowd cheering. In fact, the noise in the stadium was deafening. She glanced toward the scoreboard, which was flashing a touchdown. "We won," she said, having completely lost track of the game.

"We did," he said, but his gaze was on her and not on the game. "It's nice to be on the same side for a change, Lizzie."

And then he kissed her again, his arms sliding around her waist as he pulled her up against his chest. His mouth was hungrier now, not playful or teasing but rather demanding and insistent. His need fueled her desire. She felt like she was caught up in a fever. His lips, his mouth, his hands were all she could feel. All she could hear was the sound of his breath, and all she could feel was his hard body against her soft curves. She ran her hands up under Michael's shirt, delighting in the warmth and strength of his chest. She pushed the material up and Michael helped her strip the shirt up over his head.

She stared at his chest, swallowing hard at the male beauty: the muscled abs, the fine dark hair, the washboard stomach revealed by low riding jeans. Her mouth went dry. She felt a hunger inside of her that was shocking.

And then Michael was kissing her again, running his

hands through her hair, holding her face as he assaulted her mouth with so much passion she could barely stand up.

She lost all track of where they were—until the door to the box opened, and a cleaning person came in.

The woman let out a startled gasp and a muttered "Sorry." Then she quickly backed out of the box.

Liz stared at the door in shock, then looked back at Michael. His hair was tangled from her fingers. His mouth showed a trace of her lip gloss, and his eyes were glittering with desire. He started to reach for her again, but she put up a hand. "We can't do this here."

He looked like he wanted to argue, then his jaw tightened. "You're right."

"What was I thinking?" she muttered as he grabbed his shirt and pulled it back over his head.

"You weren't thinking—for a change. You rarely let yourself go like that, and it was great. We are good together, Liz. Better than I ever imagined. And believe me, I have imagined it more than once."

She swallowed hard, not sure how to reply to that. "You probably imagined kissing a lot of girls in high school."

"Oh, I did," he agreed, "and you were definitely on that list—until you broke my nose. Then I decided you might not be worth the pain. But I was wrong. You were worth it."

She put on her jacket and grabbed her bag. She was pretty sure she'd been crazy to hit him the first time, because to think she could have the same kiss back then was unsettling. "Let's go."

* * *

The drive back to her place took only about twenty minutes and neither of them had much to say. Liz was playing through different scenarios in her mind. When they got to her apartment, they could pick up where they left off. That would probably be really amazing. She'd never been this attracted to a man, and the way he kissed made her toes curl.

On the other hand, *this man* was her rival. How could she hook up with him? Sex would really complicate things. She'd be crossing a line. It wasn't professional.

But she didn't feel like being professional right now. She'd been putting her job first for a very long time. When did she just get to have fun?

On the other hand, she wasn't just working for herself; she was also doing it for her father, to protect his legacy. Was one night with Michael really worth jeopardizing all that?

She had a lot of questions, but she hadn't come up with any answers when Michael parked in front of her building and followed her up the stairs. He had to come inside, because he'd left his suitcase in her apartment. Now, she couldn't help wondering if that had been part of his plan.

No, that was ridiculous. Michael didn't plan. He was a live-in-the-moment kind of guy and tonight she wanted to be the kind of woman who lived in the moment, but a voice inside her head was screaming at her to be careful.

This was Michael. This was a guy who could hurt her—on a lot of levels.

She slipped her key into the lock and opened her door.

He followed her inside.

She stopped in the middle of the room, not sure what to do next. "So…"

He stared back at her, and he looked serious, far more serious than she'd ever seen him look.

After a moment, he walked slowly toward her. She felt frozen, her heart racing, her palms starting to sweat. The moment of truth had arrived.

He slid his hands through her hair, gave her another long look, an even longer kiss, and then let her go. "Goodnight,

Liz."

"You're leaving?" she asked in surprise as he let go of her.

"That's what you want, isn't it?"

She didn't know what she wanted. There was a very big part of her that wanted him to stay.

"I'm—I'm confused," she admitted.

A spark entered his eyes. "Really? That's not a word I'd ever use to describe you. You're always very sure of your purpose, your goal."

"You usually are, too," she said. "So I'm thinking that maybe you're also a little confused."

A smile played around his lips. "I keep forgetting how smart you are. Smart, beautiful and sexy." He shook his head. "You have it all, Liz."

"Then why are you leaving?"

"You didn't ask me to stay." He paused. "Are you asking me?"

She drew in a breath. "I really want to, but—"

He nodded. "But you're not. I'm not surprised. We're in the middle of a competition. And you can't forget that. What I really want to know is if that is the only reason?"

"No," she admitted. "You shake me up, you challenge my thoughts, my plans. You make me question myself. And you make me feel a little needy. I don't know what to do with all those emotions."

"You do the same to me, Liz. You've been doing it since you were a teenager."

"I really thought you were messing with me back then."

"I wasn't. I liked you. You scared the hell out of me, but I still wanted to kiss you."

"I was the nerd with paint on her clothes; you were the most popular kid in school. We did not go together then."

"What about now?"

"I don't know."

For a long moment, they just looked at each other. "I have an idea," Michael said.

"What's that?"

"Let's just hang out. No fooling around. We'll watch a movie, make popcorn, talk."

She gave him a doubtful look. "I almost ripped your clothes off less than an hour ago. You think we're going to just talk if you stay here?"

He smiled. "I can control myself. Can you? We'll take sex off the table—for tonight. What do you say?"

She hesitated but the bottom line was that she didn't want him to go. She wanted to spend more time with him, and he apparently wanted to spend more time with her. "Okay. You can stay for awhile."

Chapter Twelve

We'll take sex off the table? What the hell was wrong with him?

Michael paced around Liz's studio while she was in the bathroom, wondering where those words had come from. Temporary insanity was the only reason he could come up with. Because clearly Liz was just as attracted to him as he was to her, and a better choice of words might have had them in bed together instead of looking forward to watching movies and hanging out.

He sat down on the couch and tried to think positively. He did want to spend more time with her. And, hell, things could change, right?

Maybe if he didn't say stupid things anymore.

He turned on the television and flipped through the channels to see if there were any movies on. Perhaps a good horror film, something to get his mind off sex. Or a sappy romance. Yeah, a chick flick. She'd be happy. He'd be bored, and then he'd go home.

Liz came out of the bathroom and gave him a tentative smile as she sat down on the couch. "Anything good on?"

"There's a holiday movie called *A Thanksgiving Love Affair*. What do you think?"

She made a face at him. "It sounds cheesy and stupid."

"It's a girl movie."

"Give me the remote."

"No way, I do not give up the remote."

"It's my TV."

"Yeah, but first one with the remote wins," he said, holding it out of reach as she made a quick grab for it. "I was a quarterback. I can dodge three-hundred-pound linebackers. You really think you're going to get this away from me?"

"Well, we're not watching that movie so find something else."

He flipped through several more channels. "There's not much else on."

"Stop," she ordered.

"What?"

"It's a true crime story," she said. "I love those. They start with the murder and then show you all the suspects. It's always surprising. And I love when the detectives find just the smallest clue and make a shocking connection."

"A shocking connection?" he echoed with a smile.

"Well, they usually are," she said defensively.

"Fine, we'll watch this."

"Do you want a drink or something?" she asked. "Before it gets started?"

"I'm good."

She grabbed a blanket off the back of the couch and pulled her legs up under her.

"Hey, what if I'm cold?" he asked.

"I might be willing to share. Are you cold?"

As much as he wanted to get under that blanket with her, he knew that was a really bad idea, not if sex was off the table. "I'm okay for now."

"Suit yourself."

He turned up the volume as the story began and for the

next hour he had to admit he became riveted by the telling of a murder in a small New England town and a very unlikely suspect. During commercial breaks, Liz continually changed her mind on who was guilty, and he loved watching her try to put all the clues together. He wasn't bad at that himself, but then he'd always liked puzzles. Which was probably why he'd always liked Liz.

After the drama ended, they watched some old reruns of sitcoms, one of which had a guest appearance by one of their former high school classmates. To remember what that classmate used to look like, Liz dragged out the high school yearbooks, and they talked and laughed about mean girls, mascots, bad teachers and good friends.

"Look at you here," Liz declared, pointing to a picture of him standing at the auditorium podium. "*Most likely to be President of the United States.*"

"That was a bad call."

"It's how people saw you."

"As the most powerful man in the world?"

"Yes."

"Well they'll be disappointed when I show up at the high school reunion without the Secret Service."

"You'll still be the biggest celebrity in the room."

"What were you picked to be?"

"I was picked to be nothing, which was pretty typical of my high school experience. I wanted to be a leader, but it's hard to lead when no one wants to follow. You, on the other hand, were like the pied piper."

"Because I was selling fun, Liz. I was flash; you were substance. Teenagers don't want substance; they want flash."

She stared at him with a thoughtful gaze. "It's kind of nice that you know that." She paused. "What do you think Charlie Hayward wants?"

"I guess we'll find out."

"I have a feeling you'll be selling him fun."

"That is what he wants, Liz."

She shook her head. "No, what he wants is to sell out his park, to be the best in the world, to have people talking about him, to make money so he can keep expanding. I know how to make that happen. Do you?"

"I have some ideas and my sister does as well."

"Is she the one who's really going to come up with the plan?"

"We'll work together on it. What about your company? Are you going to bring in the partners?"

"No, I'm going to bring this account in by myself. Then the partners will have no choice but to make me a partner, too."

"Make sure there's still an actual Palmer in Damien, Falks and Palmer."

"That's right. I have to make sure they don't change the letterhead."

Michael frowned. "So this is about paper?"

"No it's about my dad's legacy. I have to protect it."

He heard the fervor in her voice. He understood that it came from a deep sense of loyalty and love for her father, but he couldn't help thinking she was running someone else's race. "What about your legacy, Liz?"

"The company will be mine, too—someday."

"Are you sure about that?"

"When I get Playworld, I'll be more sure." She paused. "My dad's former partners like to pretend that my dad never existed. But he was the heart of their firm. They were always jealous of him. My dad was the one with all the charm, bringing in all the accounts. But when he got sick, he couldn't take meetings the way he used to. Things started to fall apart for the company, so they wanted to bring in another partner, a younger guy who could do it all. My dad wanted me to take over his position. His partners fought him on it. They said I was too young, too inexperienced and that the firm needed to go in a new direction. My dad was furious. It set back his recovery because he was so angry. I hated to see him like that, so I told him I would take over the company for him. I would do what it took to become so valuable that his partners couldn't ignore me anymore or try to get me out."

"I get it, Liz, I do. I'm amazed by your loyalty to your dad, but I'm concerned about you."

"I'm fine. I'm tough. I can handle it."

He smiled at the fierce, protective light in her eyes, and he knew he couldn't change her mind. He just wished she could see the bigger picture. "What happens down the road?"

"What do you mean?"

"Let's say you do everything you intend to do. You're a partner with your dad's buddies. Is that going to make you happy? You're a creative person. Most importantly, you're your own person, and I don't see you having a good time dancing to someone else's beat."

"I can be a team player, and I will be happy, because it will make my dad happy. I love him, Michael. I can't do a lot for him, but I can do this. And so I will."

"Yeah." And now he really understood her motivation. She couldn't heal her dad, but she could make him happy, even if it was at her expense.

He was glad she'd confided in him, but a part of him also wished she hadn't. Knowing how much the Playworld account meant to her was not going to make it any easier to try to beat her. But he had his own family considerations to worry about.

"I just hope you're not pinning too much on this one account," he warned. "It's not just me you have to beat; there are two other competitors."

"I'm not worried about them. I've done some research on both Christa and Ed, and I don't think they can give Charlie what he wants."

"But you can."

"I absolutely can."

"You've never been short on confidence, Liz."

"You make that sound like an insult."

"I didn't mean it that way. It's actually a compliment. I learned a long time ago that you can't reach the top unless you believe you can. That's not all of it, of course. Desire, hunger, heart can only take you so far, but without those emotions, you can't get anywhere."

"That's true. You're a lot more eloquent now than you used to be. I remember when your poster for student body president said: *Vote for me, I'm the best*."

He laughed at the memory. "I think some cheerleader made that for me."

She rolled her eyes. "Oh, I'm sure of that. You always had a lot of help."

"You had friends who helped you."

"I did, but they were even less popular than I was, and we all know how popularity drives elections."

"It pays to be liked," he admitted.

Her gaze narrowed. "I hope with Charlie it's not going to be just about who's the most fun person or who has celebrity connections. I certainly can't compete when it comes to fame." She paused, licking her lips, a somewhat nervous look in her eyes.

"What?"

"I shouldn't say it, but..."

"But?"

"I feel like you really want to be in football, Michael. You're torn on the surface but deep down isn't that where your heart is going to take you in the end?"

"I don't know. Why are we talking about that now?"

"Because I don't want to lose to someone whose heart isn't

in the game I'm playing."

"Then you'll have to beat me," he returned, her words hitting a little below the belt.

He realized why she'd suddenly looked nervous. She'd gotten scared. After remembering how many times she'd lost to him, she'd started to worry that this bout with Playworld was going to go the same way, and she should worry, because he was good at closing a deal. "This account is just as important to me as it is to you." He paused. "Tell me something. Why did you really come to the game with me tonight?"

"I was being a friend."

"Were you? Or were you trying to see which way I was leaning, maybe even convince me to take myself out of the game?"

Her eyebrows arched in surprise, but there was also a fleeting hint of guilt in her eyes. "That's not the way it was."

He didn't believe her. "I thought I could trust you, Liz."

"Michael, you're getting this all wrong."

"Am I? Let me ask you something. Are you going to tell Charlie Hayward that I have another job offer?"

"No," she said quickly.

"It would probably give you an edge. Even if I denied it, you could raise just enough doubt in his mind to swing things your way." A rush of anger ran through him. He'd been so caught up in Liz, he'd forgotten she was his opponent. And he'd revealed far too much to her tonight. He wouldn't be so pissed off if it was just his account to lose, but his sister also had a lot at stake.

"I'm not going to tell Charlie anything," Liz said. "I don't need to cheat."

"Maybe you do," he said, getting to his feet. "Maybe the second you see that you're losing, it will just somehow slip out."

Anger sparked in her eye as she stood up. "If you didn't trust me, you shouldn't have told me your secret."

"That might have been a mistake," he conceded.

"All of this was a mistake," she declared. "I knew the second I saw you that you were going to be trouble, and I was right. I told you from the beginning that we were rivals, and we should not forget that. But you convinced me that we could be friends, too."

"I didn't have to convince you of anything. You've been attracted to me since you were a teenager."

"You should go home."

"I am going home." He grabbed his suitcase, but when he got to the doorway he paused. "Just so you know, when it comes to you and me, sex is never off the table."

"You're crazy," she declared. "I don't even like you right now."

"Well, I don't like you much, either. But I still want you and you still want me. And in the end, we're going to do something about it."

"No, we're not." She walked across the room, pushed him into the hallway and slammed the door.

It felt very much like the punch to the nose he'd taken all those years ago.

* * *

After Michael left, Liz felt incredibly frustrated and worked up. They'd been having a good time and then everything had gone wildly off track. She didn't really know how it had happened. Actually, she did know. She'd gotten super competitive.

While she would never tell Charlie Hayward about Michael's football opportunities, she had used her knowledge of his other job offer to make him question his intentions. Was that really wrong?

She was just stating the obvious. If he left his sister's agency to go back to football, then how could he possibly be the right person to run the Playworld account?

She paced around the room, trying to burn off the rush of adrenaline that was fueled not only by their argument, but also by his distrust of her, and maybe just a little sexual frustration.

His last comment about sex never being off the table still rang through her head, and as much as she didn't like him right now, her body was singing another restless tune.

Her phone buzzed on the coffee table. As she reached for it, she thought it might be Michael, but it was a text from Julie asking her if she'd made it onto the roller coaster and if she was still alive.

She sat down on the couch, her anger dissipating as the reminder of the roller coaster also brought back the memory of Michael holding her hand, talking her through it. Damn him for being a nicer competitor than she was.

She picked up the phone and called Julie back.

"Oh, hey," Julie said. "I guess this means you are alive."

"I am. I made it on the ride."

"Congratulations. You must feel pretty good about that."

"I do," she said, her eyes blurring with moisture.

"You sound funny. What's wrong?"

She let out a sigh. "I've messed everything up, Julie."

"What are you talking about—the account?"

"No, not the account—*him*."

"Are we talking about Michael? Oh my God, did you sleep with him?"

"No, I didn't. But I should have slept with him. Then my mouth might not have gotten me into trouble." She paused. "I think I hurt him."

"Did you punch him again?"

Her laugh turned into a sob. "Not literally, but I got too

competitive. And I used something he told me against him. I don't know why I did it. We were having fun. But then we started talking about the account, and that little beast inside of me came out. I just..." She didn't even know how to explain what she had done. "I just blew it."

"You like him, don't you?" Julie asked.

Her hand tightened around the phone. "I do," she admitted. "I think I have all along."

"I know you have. He only bothered you so much in high school, because you had a big crush on him."

"But I always knew I could never really have him."

"I'm coming over," Julie said.

"You don't have to do that. It's almost midnight."

"I'll be in there in fifteen minutes. I'll bring ice cream."

"You're a good friend."

"You'd do it for me—especially if I'd just realized I'd fallen in love."

Her stomach turned over at Julie's words. "I'm not in love with him," she said, but Julie had already ended the call. "I'm not in love with him," she repeated. "Am I?"

Chapter Thirteen

After talking out her problems with Julie, Liz had finally gone to bed around two. When she got up to go into the office on Tuesday morning she was definitely feeling the effects of a sleepless night. She set her bag on the counter behind her desk, sat down and turned on her computer. While it was starting up, she looked around the room, feeling like she'd been gone for a year instead of a couple of days. The office she'd spent most of her life in for the past year felt strange and unfamiliar. And while normally she'd always been happy to get to work, today she felt restless.

Forcing those feelings away, she opened the Playworld account on her computer and ordered herself to get to work. She might not know how to handle sexy men, but she did know how to put together a strong PR campaign; her dad had taught her well.

She started with the basics and then moved into specific campaigns and strategies. As she typed, she could hear her dad's voice in her head, reminding her of what was important and that made her feel even closer to him. She was on the right track, she thought.

Two hours later, she printed out her proposal and read through it.

It was good. But it was missing something.

Now the voice in her head belonged to Charlie Hayward. She could hear his passion as he talked about his dream, about creating a world that changed people's lives, even if only for a day.

Was she giving him what he wanted?

Her proposal was solid. It was exactly the kind of pitch that Damien, Falks and Palmer always made and always won. And as she looked at all the different areas of the campaign—promotion, marketing, advertising, media—she knew there was no way the other agencies could match the resources of her company. She felt a renewed surge of confidence that she could bring home a win.

A knock at her door lifted her gaze. Brian Hargrove stepped into her office. The tall, handsome hotshot always brought a sick, wary feeling to her stomach, and today was no exception. She and Brian had joined the firm at the same time. But at that time, her father had still occupied an office and she'd been the heir apparent. Once her dad had left, Brian had become the boy wonder to Bill Falks and Howard Damien. Only one of them was going to make partner in the next year, and she knew that if she didn't have Playworld in her pocket, it would not be her.

"How's it going?" Brian picked up the proposal and scanned the first page. "Interesting."

"It's just preliminary," she said, grabbing the paper out of his hand. "What do you want?"

"I called you yesterday."

"I was busy."

"Well, you should have called me back. I hate to be the one to tell you this, Liz, but there have been some developments since you left the office, and Bill and Howard thought you might receive the information better if it came from me."

Her stomach twisted into a knot. "Just spit it out, Brian. Judging by the gloating gleam in your eyes, it's something about you."

"You're not a good loser, Liz."

"Well, I don't usually lose," she countered. "So I don't have a lot of practice."

"Looks like you're about to get some practice. I was made partner yesterday."

She stared at him in shock. "That's impossible. I'm bringing in Playworld, and that's worth millions to this company."

"Well, you haven't brought it in yet. And this weekend I signed up Triple Media Threat for a five year, multi-million-dollar deal."

She was truly stunned by his announcement. She had had no idea the huge media company had been in talks with her agency, which just went to show just how far out of the inner circle she was. "I can't believe I didn't know you were going after it."

"They wanted to work quietly."

"Who's they?"

"Triple Media, of course."

"And Bill and Howard?"

"They go with the client. You know that."

"Well…Congratulations." It was hard to get the word out, but what choice did she have? "That's quite a coup."

"Interesting choice of words."

"More like accurate," she said, unable to hide the bitterness in her voice.

"Come on, Liz. This isn't your dad's company anymore. Damien and Falks are moving in a new direction. Your dad was old school. Frankly, in trying to live up to him, you're old school, too."

"That's not true. My father was a brilliant promotional

specialist."

"Maybe ten years ago, but not now. You have good ideas, but you're afraid to step outside your father's box. Everyone sees that but you. You need to change or you need to move on." He shrugged. "Sorry if that's harsh. But I know you appreciate it when people are direct. Oh, and Bill wants me to review the Playworld pitch before you present."

"I don't need your opinion. You don't know anything about Playworld."

"I know how to run a campaign, and I'm a partner, so you don't really have a say, Liz. Email me your presentation. We can talk it over tomorrow."

She blew out a breath as he left her office, her head spinning. She couldn't believe everything that had happened behind her back. She hadn't known about Triple Media. She hadn't known that Brian was in line for partner. She hadn't known anything. And Bill had stood here in her office on Friday and never said a word.

Brian had taken the partner spot that she wanted, and there was nothing she could do about it. She sat back in her chair, mulling over what else Brian had said. He'd told her that her ideas were behind the times, but her ideas were solid— weren't they?

Or was she just following her dad's lead, trying to keep his visions alive, even if they didn't completely make sense anymore?

She stared down at her presentation notes. And she knew now exactly what was missing—heart, fire, creativity—all the things that Charlie wanted. Her rational voice tried to argue that all that passion was great, but her proposal still needed substance.

That thought took her back to her conversation with Michael when he'd called himself the flash and her the substance. Was that it? Was she always doomed to be the boring player on a losing side?

Frowning, she got up and paced around her office.

And then, she got pissed. Did the partners honestly think she was just going to hand them Playworld on a silver platter and work like a dutiful soldier for people who didn't believe in her anymore?

Grabbing her bag, she headed out the door. She didn't know the answer to her problems, but she did know one thing. She needed to breathe, to think, to come up with a plan, and she could not take one more second inside the office that had been designed to keep her in her place, to make her feel small. She wasn't small. She was a fighter, and she was not done yet.

She just had to figure out what she was really fighting for.

* * *

Michael spent two hours at the office, long enough to fill in his sister Erica and Kent Richards, another Account Executive, on his assessment of what Charlie Hayward was looking for in the pitch to be made on Thursday. After a long brainstorming session, Erica had told him that she and Kent would come up with campaign plan. Central to that plan would be using his celebrity contacts in a creative way.

With that conference over, Michael felt at loose ends. He liked being the front guy, taking the meetings, making the pitch, but the actual work—that was obviously not going to be done by him. Erica seemed good with the division of labor, and he'd been okay with it, too, until now—until he'd talked to Hank, gone to a football game, and let Liz Palmer into his head.

Too restless to stay in the office, he jumped in his truck and headed out of the city. In his hurry to get the hell away from Liz the night before, he'd forgotten to give her the signed jersey and hat he'd gotten for her dad. But he didn't need to give it to her to deliver; he could take it to Palo Alto himself. A drive would be good for his head, and then he wouldn't have to see her again.

At least, he wouldn't have to see her until Thursday when there was a very good chance he'd run into her, because his pitch was right before hers.

After talking to Erica and Kent, he had even more confidence that he could sell their firm to Charlie, because he knew exactly what made the man tick. He was on his way to winning the Playworld account. He should feel good about that.

But he couldn't help thinking he was going to crush Liz.

It wasn't like high school when it didn't really matter who ended up homeroom monitor or student body president. Her reasons for needing to win were deep and emotional, and he felt her pain and her terror at the thought of losing her dad, her anchor. He knew that her commitment to her father's firm was more about that than anything else. And he shouldn't have goaded her the night before.

Not that she hadn't swung right back at him, challenging his motives, his desire to even be in PR, and making him wonder if he was cheating to try to win an account that he probably would only end up doing ten percent of the work on once it came to the agency.

Damn Liz. She always got under his skin.

Usually, because she was right.

Because her words had stung, he'd hit back at her, accusing of her something he knew she'd never do—tell Charlie he had another job opportunity. Liz liked to win, but she didn't play dirty. Not once, in all of their battles, had she ever taken the cheap shot.

He'd hurt her with the accusation.

Sighing, he hit his fist against the steering wheel. How the hell had the evening gone from great to terrible so fast? He always seemed to screw things up with Liz. And that bothered him because she was important. She mattered. She always had. She'd stuck in his head all the years they'd been apart.

He could barely remember the other women he'd dated. They'd all been attractive, fun, ready for a good time, and he'd had a lot of good times, but none of those women had ever challenged him in the way Liz did. No one had ever brought out the side of him that she did, the side that was more serious, that wanted to make something of his life.

He had been making something of his life, but now he was starting over. And each new step he took forward now seemed more uncertain than the last.

So he wouldn't take any steps for the rest of the day; he'd just drive. And think. And think some more.

By the time he arrived at Liz's parents' house in Palo Alto he was tired of the thoughts rolling around in his head and more than happy to get out of the truck. He rang the bell and a moment later, Liz's mom opened the door.

She gave him a happy smile of surprise. "Michael. I didn't expect you." She looked past him. "Is Liz with you?"

"No, she's not. I brought something for Ron. I was at the Blackhawks game last night, and my friend Keith Saxton signed a jersey and a hat for him. He wrote a little message, too."

"Oh my goodness. That is so wonderful and amazing. Ron loves Keith Saxton. He's one of his favorite players—well, after you, of course."

He smiled as she quickly backtracked. "You don't need to explain. I'm not a player anymore."

"Well, come on in."

"I don't want to disturb him."

"You won't be. He's just reading some book about World War Two. I know he'd love the company."

"Sure." He followed her into the house and down the hall

to the family room.

Ron looked up and quickly brought his recliner into a sitting position. "Hello, Michael."

"Hi. I was at the Blackhawks' game last night. I brought you these." He handed the hat and jersey to Ron and then sat down on the couch.

"Are you kidding?" Ron asked in amazement.

"Saxton wrote a note to you," Joan added.

"Stay strong. We're rooting for you," Ron read. He cleared his throat and looked back at Michael. "This is great. Thank you."

"You're welcome."

"Can I get you something to drink, Michael?"

"No, I'm fine."

"I'll let you two chat," Joan said.

As Joan left the room, Michael turned back to Ron. "What did you think of the game last night?"

"I think they miss you as quarterback. The defense is on the mark, but the offense barely pulled it out. If it hadn't been for that penalty in the fourth quarter, the outcome could have been different."

"Absolutely, they dodged a bullet."

Ron tilted his head, giving him a thoughtful look. "Do you miss it, Michael?"

"More than I ever thought I would," he admitted. "Football was my life for a long time. I woke up thinking about plays and went to bed thinking about plays. I almost hated to sleep."

"That's what it takes to be good at something. You have to want it bad. Have you ever thought about coaching?"

His gaze narrowed. "Did Liz talk to you?"

"About what?" Ron asked, a question in his eyes.

"Nothing." He ran a hand through his hair, then said, "I have recently been considering the idea of coaching. The past year I thought it would be easier for me to be done with football in every possible way. Now, I'm not so sure."

"You're a young man. You have a lot of life to live. You lost the ability to play the game you loved on a professional level, but there's something else you're going to love doing. You just have to figure out what that is. The most important thing is to do whatever you do well, put your heart and soul into it. Sometimes, we end up in careers we never imagined. You'd be surprised what can get your heart pumping. It's not always what you expect."

"Did that happen to you? Did you end up in a career you hadn't planned on?" he asked curiously.

"Sure. What little boy dreams of running a PR company? I wanted to be a football player, too, but I just wasn't good enough. I played high school ball and that was it. Then I went into music. I started playing the drums for my friend's band. By the time I was out of college, I was playing gigs all around Los Angeles."

"I had no idea," he said in amazement.

"Music was a blast, but I was smart enough to know it didn't pay the bills. That's when I started thinking about a real job. I interned at a media company and found out I was great at marketing, visualizing promotions and figuring out what would persuade someone to buy something. And that's how I got into PR. I built a great company."

"You certainly did that. And now Liz is following in your footsteps."

"It was great when Liz came into the company. She became my sounding board, the one person I could really trust. And she was as good as I was."

As Ron spoke, Michael wondered if Ron had ever realized just how determined Liz was to save his company for him.

"Liz told me she's working hard to make partner."

Ron frowned. "Yeah, but she has an uphill battle in front of her. I know she loves a challenge, and she's as stubborn as they come, sometimes a little too stubborn. I wish—"

"Michael?" Liz interrupted. "What are you doing here?"

Michael turned around to see Liz standing in the doorway, anger in her eyes. "I brought your father the jersey and the hat," he explained.

"Oh. I forgot I left them in your truck."

"I was down this way anyway. Why aren't you at work?"

"Yes, why aren't you at work?" Ron echoed.

"I wanted to talk to you, Dad." She walked across the room and kissed her father on the forehead. "How are you feeling today?"

"I'm doing all right. It's nice to have so much company. What did you want to talk to me about?"

Liz glanced at Michael.

"Do you want me to go?" he asked.

She hesitated, then shrugged. "It doesn't matter." She turned her gaze back to her father. "I have to tell you something, Dad. Brian was made partner today. Apparently, he brought in Triple Media Threat over the weekend. Even if I get Playworld, I probably won't get a partnership until next year."

"Really? I'm sorry to hear that."

"I didn't even know we were going after Triple Media. They've really kept me out of the loop."

"Well, what can you do?" Ron said, disappointment in his weary eyes.

"Maybe Bill and Howard will change their minds when they see the dollars coming in for Playworld. If I get it, of course," she added, giving Michael a quick glance. "That's still to be determined."

"I'm going to take off," Michael said, not wanting to get in the middle of their private conversation.

"No need to rush off," Ron said quickly.

"I have an appointment," he said.

"Thanks again for the jersey and the hat."

"I'm glad you like them." He got up and shook Ron's hand.

"I'll walk you out," Liz said, surprising him with the offer.

They didn't speak until they got to his truck. Then Liz surprised him again.

"I'm sorry," she said.

"For what exactly?"

"For what I said last night. Sometimes when I start to feel backed into a corner, I come out swinging."

He smiled. "Both literally and metaphorically."

"You're never going to forget that, are you?"

"I'm reminded every time I look in the mirror."

"Anyway—"

"Why did you feel backed into a corner?" he interrupted. "We were just talking."

"I think it was looking at the yearbook that triggered my insecurity. I started remembering how you always beat me, and I had a little panic attack."

He appreciated how candid she was being. "I get it. I should apologize, too."

"No, you were right, Michael. Everything you said about me was true. I can't save my dad's life, so I'm trying to save his company, but the truth is I can't do that, either. I saw that today. I'll never be able to get the power that he had."

"Maybe that's all right, Liz. Some things run their course. Careers change. Your dad was just saying that to me."

She gave him a quizzical look. "What do you mean? What were you talking about?"

"We were talking about football, and he mentioned that he once wanted to play, then realized he wasn't good enough. Then he tried music and realized he still needed to make money. So he found something he was really good at, but it wasn't what he imagined. He told me I should keep my mind open."

She stared back at him, and he couldn't tell what she was thinking.

"What?" he asked.

"I forgot that my dad used to drum. He used to play when I was little, but then he got so involved in building his company, he let that go."

"He found a new dream."

"I guess he did."

Her gaze met his, and his gut tightened. He felt such an emotional pull towards her. He wanted to kiss her and hold her and comfort her after what had obviously been a bad morning, but in her eyes, he was the enemy. He really wanted another title.

"Michael." She said his name with a breathless murmur, then gave a helpless shake of her head. "I don't know what we're doing."

"We're just standing on a sidewalk."

"I know, but—"

"But it's what is going on in your head that worries you."

"Exactly."

"I don't have any answers," he admitted. "I think we're good together, but there's always something between us, something to win, something to lose… Until that changes—"

"We just stand on the sidewalk," she said.

"Well, at least we know we can finish each other's sentences," he said lightly.

His phone buzzed, and he pulled it out of his pocket, seeing a text from Erica. She had a new idea she wanted to run by him. "I better take this."

"Of course. Thanks for bringing the jersey down. That was really thoughtful of you, Michael."

"It wasn't a big deal. I guess I'll see you at Playworld. May the best man—or woman—win."

Chapter Fourteen

By late Wednesday afternoon, Liz wasn't thinking so much about winning as about quitting. After sending her proposal to Brian and the other partners, she'd received a detailed critique of just about every aspect of her plan. It was clear that no one had any confidence in her, and now she was having a few doubts herself.

After she'd left Michael yesterday, she'd gone back into her parents' house and asked her dad to tell her about his music career again. She'd spent the afternoon with her mom and dad, laughing and listening to their stories—stories she'd heard dozens of times before, but somehow she'd forgotten most of them. In fact, listening to her dad talk about his dream of making the cover of *Rolling Stone* had made her realize that he had had other passions besides this company.

Which got her to thinking…

Michael had asked her if she was planning to spend her whole life walking in her dad's footsteps.

Brian had told her she thought just like her dad, but that was old-fashioned thinking. She needed to become more cutting-edge.

Bill and Howard had made her feel like the uninvited guest at a very long birthday party.

So what the hell was she fighting for?

She'd thought saving her dad's company would make him happy, give him something to smile about, but the truth was the happiest she'd seen him in recent months had been Sunday when they'd all watched football together as a family and yesterday when he'd told her about his life as a drummer.

Had the company become less important in his mind now that he's retired, and she'd somehow missed that?

She frowned at the thought. She hadn't made up his desire to have her protect his interests, but maybe they were both starting to realize that they couldn't hang on to a past that was in truth already gone.

She pushed aside Brian's notes and pulled the sketches of Playworld out of her bag. As she looked at her drawings, she suddenly knew exactly what she had to do.

* * *

Michael got to Playworld thirty minutes before his presentation on Thursday was scheduled to begin. He had a slide show ready to go on his laptop, and he'd gone over strategy with Erica and Kent long into the night. He was ready to make his pitch. More than ready. He felt the excitement he normally felt before a football game, and Liz's dad's words rang through his head. *You'd be surprised at what can get your heart pumping.*

He was surprised. He'd taken the job with Erica because he honestly hadn't known what else to do and at that point in his life, any job was as good as another. With football off the table, what did it matter what he did?

But it did matter. He didn't want to just mark the days off the calendar. He wanted to live his life, and whatever he was going to do, he wanted to do it well.

He glanced down at his watch, thinking Liz was probably on her way.

He hadn't talked to her since he'd left her at her father's house on Tuesday afternoon. There was nothing more to say until they got this damn competition out from between them. Then he was going to have a lot to say. Unfortunately, what he said would depend on the outcome of this pitch.

If Liz lost, she'd take it hard and probably blame him for ruining her life, but he'd never thrown a game, and he wasn't going to start now. He also knew that Liz didn't want to win by default. She wanted to beat him, and if she did, he'd be the first to congratulate her.

A woman's voice rang out, and he got to his feet. Christa came through the double doors leading into the executive offices. She appeared quite happy. Maybe this competition wasn't just between him and Liz.

"It looks like things went well," he said, noticing that not only had Christa brought some poster boards with her, she was also showing off a lot of cleavage. He couldn't blame her for using every weapon she had. Unfortunately, that weapon was not in his arsenal.

"It went amazingly well," she said. "Charlie is such a flirt. I think he'd really enjoy working with me."

"I imagine a lot of men would like working with you," he said dryly.

"You could always jump ship and join my firm. We could be good together—both in and out of the office."

"That's a tempting offer, but I'm happy where I am."

"Well, good luck. You're going to need it."

"Mr. Stafford?" the receptionist said. "You can go in now."

He nodded and grabbed his materials. He felt like he was going into the playoffs and sudden death. He had one play. Win or lose, there wasn't going to be a second chance.

* * *

Liz felt a lot more relaxed for her second meeting at Playworld than she had for the first, which was surprising, since today was going to determine her future for at least the next year. Instead of grimacing at the childlike atmosphere, she embraced it, talking back to the talking chair and enjoying a fun puzzle on the table in front of her. She wasn't going to stress over her pitch. She knew what she had to do. She had it under control, and it was the first time in a very long time that she'd felt that way.

She looked up as Michael came through the doors. He looked confident but also tired.

His expression brightened when he saw her. "Lizzie."

The nickname only made her smile. She felt more like Lizzie now than she had last week. "Did you knock his socks off?"

"I made my pitch. He seemed receptive, excited at times, but Charlie doesn't give much away. He's definitely listening to every detail though."

"I'm sure you did a good job, Michael. You always do." She took a deep breath. "I guess it's my turn."

"I'm going to wait for you."

"Really?" she asked, surprised by the offer.

"Yes. I want to ride the Ferris wheel with you. You gave me a rain check, remember?"

"All right. You've got a deal."

"And whatever happens—"

"Will happen," she finished.

He grinned. "I was going to say that. You know, you seem remarkably calm."

"I had an epiphany yesterday."

"Care to share?"

"Not right now. I better go."

"Watch out for the quicksand, Lizzie."

"Don't worry. I know exactly where to step."

* * *

While Liz was making her pitch, Michael headed out to the parking lot to drop off his computer and presentation materials. Then he grabbed a coffee on his way back into the park and sat down on a bench outside of the castle. He pulled out his phone to call Erica, knowing she was eagerly awaiting the results of his meeting.

"Tell me it was good, Michael," she said, not bothering to start with *hello*.

"It was good. Charlie liked a lot of our ideas. However, he did question the ability of our young firm to reach the national media."

"But we have *your* connections."

"Which are primarily in sports."

"Do you think it's going to be a deal breaker?"

"I honestly don't know. Charlie and I had a great talk. I understand his vision and how he wants to present himself to the world, and I think we can do a great job for him. But I didn't see the other presentations so I have no idea what we're up against."

"Can you get any information out of Liz?"

"I'm not going to ask her. It doesn't matter what she thinks anyway. It's all up to Charlie."

"Okay. Thanks for all your hard work, Michael. We wouldn't have even been invited to pitch if Charlie hadn't been intrigued by you, so you got us in the door. Whatever happens next, I'll know we did our best. I'll talk to you tomorrow."

"See you then." He blew out a breath. Then he dialed another number. "Hank, it's Michael. Call me back when you get a chance. I've made a decision."

He sat down on the bench and opened up his emails. He

might as well work on some of the other projects Erica had assigned to him.

An hour later, Liz walked out of the castle. Relief flitted through her eyes when she saw him.

"I thought you might have changed your mind and gone home," she said.

"Not a chance. I just needed to sit someplace where the furniture didn't talk to me."

"Good point." She sat down next to him on the bench and let out a breath. "So that's done."

"Should I ask how it went?"

"I think it went well," she said carefully.

He smiled. "Christa gave me more than that."

"Really? What did Christa say?"

"That Charlie was a big flirt and she thought he'd enjoy working with her. She was dressed to seduce, so he had some interesting scenery to look at."

"Using sex to win seems kind of cheap."

"It might work."

"I don't think so."

"You think you pulled it off, don't you?" he asked, seeing the gleam in her eyes.

"I honestly don't know."

"You seem remarkably serene about it all."

"Well, it's out of my hands now, and—"

"And you had an epiphany. That's what you said before. Are you going to tell me what it was?"

She smiled. "I want to tell you about it, but the sun is already setting. Look at the sky. It's purple, pink and orange all at the same time. I think we'll have a better view from the top of the Ferris wheel. And you promised me a ride."

There was definitely something different about Liz, but she was clearly not going to talk until she was ready.

As they walked across the park, he impulsively took Liz's

hand in his, and he was happy when she didn't pull away, even happier when she gave him a smile that made his heart beat faster.

The line for the Ferris wheel was short, and within minutes they were entering their own private gondola, ready to take them on a twenty-minute ride on one of the tallest Ferris wheels in the world.

"This ride doesn't bother you?" Michael asked as they sat on opposites sides of the Gondola.

"It goes really slow, and I'm comfortable having all the glass around me."

"Good to hear. So tell me what's going on with you, Liz. You're different, and I want to know why."

She gave him a happy smile. "It's unusual for you *not* to be able to read my mind. I think I like being mysterious."

"Come on, you're killing me here."

"Fine. I realized yesterday when I was going over all the suggestions from my bosses that there was no way I could win the Playworld account and make them happy at the same time. What they wanted wasn't what Charlie wanted."

"But you just said that you gave Charlie a great presentation."

"I did, but in doing so I had to go against what my partners asked me to present. Which means they're not going to be happy that I included points that they asked me to take out."

"They'll be happy if you win. Money can buy a lot of forgiveness."

"Maybe. I didn't really have a choice. They wouldn't listen to me when I told them what kind of campaign Charlie was looking for. And I knew I couldn't waste Charlie's time or my own by presenting what they came up with. So I had to make a decision."

"Which was what?"

"To shoot the moon. I put in everything I thought would make a great campaign. I held nothing back. I even included some of my sketches."

His stomach began to feel a little sick, because it was very clear that Liz had probably outdone herself and given Charlie far beyond what he and Erica had come up with. The truth was Liz had more experience than anyone at Erica's very young company. And she'd learned from her dad, who'd been one of the best.

"Michael?"

He looked into her eyes, realizing he'd drifted off. "Sorry, I was just thinking that you probably won this."

Her gaze turned more somber. "I don't know. I just focused on giving Charlie the best of what I knew. It wasn't about beating you, Michael."

"Hey, you don't have to explain anything. I fully expected you to bring your best game. I would have been disappointed if you hadn't. If I'm going to get beat, I want it to be by the best, and I think that might be you, Liz."

"We'll find out tomorrow. I told Charlie when I was leaving that no matter what he decided, I was really happy he allowed me to spend time in his park and make the pitch, because the last few days have been life-changing. I rediscovered my dreams, my desire to draw and create. I found myself again. And to be honest it wasn't just this park that did that; it was you, too." She paused and gave him a somewhat tender smile that made his heart flip over in his chest. "You made me remember the girl I used to be, and even though there were things about that girl I didn't like, there were a lot of other things I did like. I used to be independent, Michael. I prided myself on not being a follower. But that's what I became when I followed my dad into his company and then I had to follow everyone else after he left. That's why I couldn't give Charlie the presentation that my company wanted me to do. It was time to take a stand."

"Good for you. I kind of wish you'd had your epiphany tomorrow, but…"

She laughed. "You haven't lost yet. I can remember a lot of times when I thought you were going down only to see your name pop up in the win column. So I'm not going to count on anything until we hear from Charlie." She paused, giving him a more serious look. "Will you hate me if I win?"

"Will you hate me?" he countered.

"In high school, I used to try to hate you; it never really worked. Somehow, I doubt this time would be any different."

"Even though the stakes are higher? This win is for your dad as much as it's for you, if not more."

"That's true. But if you win, then you deserve it."

"I feel the same way," he said, but he couldn't help wondering if she'd really have that calm reaction in the end. Right now, she probably thought she had it wrapped up and losing wasn't going to be an issue.

Liz let out a sigh and looked around. "It is beautiful up here."

He followed her gaze as their gondola crested the top peak of the wheel. The amazing colors of the sky painted a bright picture that continued to change as the sun sunk lower in the sky and the moon began to rise. He could see for miles, and he'd always been one to be inspired by a view, by the possibilities.

But he found himself looking away from the landscape and back at the woman who was inspiring him in a lot of other ways.

He got up and sat down next to her.

She grabbed on to the rail with a nervous smile. "Uh, isn't this going to throw us off balance?"

He laughed. "No, but this might." He touched her mouth with his, tenderly at first, wanting to savor her soft lips, her sweet taste, but a rush of desire sent the kiss into overdrive and he was happy when Liz parted her lips and invited him inside. She was sexy and sweet, cool and fiery all at the same time. She was the girl who'd always tempted him to want more, to be better, to think bigger. Their battles had driven him to achieve more than he ever would have achieved on his own. And it was because of her.

His Lizzie.

He kissed her until their gondola came around for a stop, and then he asked the attendant if they could take another spin. The young woman laughed and said, "Why not?"

"You're crazy," Liz said as they began another ascent.

"You weren't ready to get off this ride, were you?"

She looked back at him. "No, I wasn't. In fact, I don't know if I'm ever going to be able to get off this ride with you, Michael."

His heart jumped again. "I've been wondering the same thing."

Chapter Fifteen

Liz arrived at Playworld's executive offices at noon on Friday. Charlie had called first thing in the morning announcing he was ready to make a decision. Michael was already in the lobby when she walked in. He smiled and walked across the room to give her a hug.

"Hey," he said. "I guess it's the moment of truth."

"I guess so."

She nodded, feeling revved up for a lot of different reasons. After she and Michael had finally gotten off the Ferris wheel the night before, they'd gotten dinner together. They'd talked about nothing important, either instinctively or deliberately staying away from touchy subjects like family and career.

After dinner, they'd made out a little by her car and then parted ways to drive back to the city. For some reason neither one of them had pushed to keep the evening going, even though things were going incredibly well. But she wanted the competition to be over before they got even closer. Despite the fact that they'd both said they could take the loss, who knew how either of them would feel when it actually happened?

"Where's Christa or Ed?" she asked.

"Haven't seen them. Maybe this means we're the final two."

"It would seem appropriate if it came down to the two of us."

He gazed back at her as if he wanted to say something, but then decided against it.

"What?" she prodded.

"Nothing. Let's get this over with."

He seemed tense for a man who was usually cool and confident.

"You're nervous," she said.

"And you're not?"

"Oh, no, my stomach is definitely doing somersaults."

"I feel the same way. If this was just about me…"

"I know. It's harder to lose when the loss affects someone else."

The receptionist interrupted their conversation. "You can go down the hall. Mr. Hayward is ready for you."

She had to fight the urge to take Michael's hand. They weren't together in this, she reminded herself. They were two opponents about to find out who would be the victor.

Charlie stood up as they entered his office. He gave them both a welcoming smile and waved them into the two chairs in front of his desk.

"Miss Palmer, Mr. Stanford, you both delivered excellent presentations yesterday."

Liz drew in a breath, wishing he didn't feel the need to bother with compliments. She just wanted him to get on with it.

"I called you here together, because I wanted you both to hear my thought process. Your firms each have strengths and weaknesses," Charlie continued. "And quite honestly, while I thought I had made a decision this morning, that changed about fifteen minutes ago. Neither one of you made this an easy choice. First of all, I'd like to say that the other two agencies were eliminated yesterday. Neither one understood or gave me what I was looking for."

Charlie directed his gaze to Michael. "You have celebrity connections that no one else has. But celebrities only get me so far, and your firm is young and not as experienced. Still, I liked your campaign and thought it showed great promise. You understand what I want for this park, which is very much like a child to me. That sounds ridiculous, but it's how I feel."

Charlie then turned his gaze to Liz. "You presented what appeared to me to be almost two disparate campaigns. You blended them together as skillfully as you could, but there was a disconnect in there, and I couldn't help wondering why. It puzzled me most of the night, in fact."

She could tell him why but she didn't want to get into office politics.

Sitting back in his chair, Charlie rubbed his jaw, his gaze still on Liz. "Fifteen minutes ago, I got a call from one of the new partners in your firm, Brian Hargrove."

Now, she felt sick. What the hell had Brian been thinking?

"Mr. Hargrove said he wanted to make sure that I understood how much your agency wanted my business and that if I wasn't comfortable with anything in your presentation, they would be happy to change it. In fact, he would be happy to meet with me personally. He told me that your father is ill and that in dealing with his health issues, you may not have as much time to commit to my account as you wish."

"Mr. Hayward, I assure you—"

He cut her off with a wave of his hand. "Let me finish. It became quite clear to me during our conversation that your firm does not want you to run my account, Miss Palmer."

How could she argue with that? Still, she had to try. "When I commit to a job, I go all in. I don't quit, and I don't allow distractions to get in the way of my job. My father's health is an ongoing issue, but I'm not his primary caregiver, and he's better at the moment."

"I have no doubt that you would try to do your best for me," Charlie said. "But I don't think your firm will let you do your best for me. Judging by the conversation with Mr. Hargrove, I suspect I will find my company embroiled in your agency politics, which is not what I need or desire. Therefore, I've decided to award the account to Mr. Stafford's firm."

She swallowed hard as a multitude of emotions ran through her. She'd lost to Michael—*again*!

She'd really thought she'd had it this time. Her proposal was better than his, but Brian Hargrove had stepped in, shot his mouth off and blown everything.

"Congratulations, Michael," she said, forcing the word out.

Michael gave her a concerned look. "Thanks."

She looked at Charlie. "I know Michael and his firm will do a good job for you."

"I am sorry, Miss Palmer. I liked your ideas a lot. I was leaning in your direction, but I can't let my company get caught in the middle of a war."

"I understand."

"Do you remember what you said to me when you left yesterday—about how the park had changed your life, made you remember who you used to be?" Charlie asked.

"Yes."

"Well, if you don't mind some unwanted advice, I'd suggest you think about whether your firm is really where you want to be now. They tried to impress me by bringing in the big guns, but I always wanted you. I knew, like your father, that you would be honest, creative, and ethical. And it's quite clear to me that your father's former company treads a fine line in some of those areas."

"Things have changed a lot since my father left the firm."

"After I spoke to Mr. Hargrove, I realized why your

presentation felt like it had two parts. One was theirs and one was yours, wasn't it?"

"Yes. They didn't want me to present my side, but I couldn't waste your time without giving you my best." She got to her feet. "I do very much appreciate the opportunity to pitch. Thank you for that. I'm going to go now and let you two talk strategy."

She turned and left the room without giving Michael another glance. She couldn't look at him right now. She wanted to be happy for him, but she was too caught up in the emotion of losing and the shock of how the firm had sold her out.

Walking quickly out of the building, she didn't slow her pace until she reached her car. Once inside, she sat back and drew in a couple of deep breaths as she looked at the flying flags surrounding the park. She would have loved to work on this account. But it wasn't going to be hers. And truthfully, deep down inside, she knew that even if she'd gotten the account, Brian and the other partners would have been on her every second to do things their way.

She'd told Michael yesterday that she'd had an epiphany—that she'd realized she could cower in the corner or follow blindly like a good soldier. She had to take charge of her life and her career.

Picking up her phone, she called Brian. "Nice move calling Mr. Hayward," she said.

"I assume that means we got the account."

She found herself smiling at the cocky note in his voice. "He was going to give us the account, until you called. He said he couldn't hire a firm that didn't support its own employees and that it was clear to him that if he went with us because he wanted me, he was not going to get me. So, no, Brian, we didn't get the account. Mr. Hayward's millions are going to another firm."

"That's a bunch of bullshit, Liz, a nice story to cover up the fact that you lost. In the end, that's all Bill and Howard are going to care about. You lost a huge account for the firm. Don't be surprised if your office doesn't end up in a closet."

"Oh, that's not going to happen," she said.

"Your dad can't protect you anymore."

"I don't need him to protect me." She hung up the phone before she could say the words that were hovering on her tongue—*I quit*. She wasn't going to give Brian the satisfaction of taking her resignation. No, if she were going to change her life, she would do it the right way.

* * *

Michael rushed out of the office a good thirty minutes after Liz had left, hoping he'd find her waiting for him outside. But she was gone.

Of course she was gone. She'd lost to him again.

Even though she'd told him yesterday she could handle whatever happened, clearly the loss hurt—a lot. Not just for her but for her dad. And the fact that he'd played a part in hurting her didn't sit well. But her loss wasn't totally his fault. Liz's own company had taken her down. If the partner at her firm hadn't called Charlie, Liz would be celebrating and he'd be dealing with how to break the bad news to his sister.

Which reminded him that he needed to call his sister. He pulled out his phone.

Erica answered on the first ring. "Well?"

"We got it," he said, still amazed he was bringing her such fantastic news.

"I can't believe it. I was hoping, but I really thought it would go to Damien, Falks and Palmer."

"Charlie was leaning that way, but in the end he went with us."

"This is freaking fantastic."

"It is. I'm leaving now. I'll bring champagne to the office. Tell everyone to be ready to celebrate in a few hours."

"Are you kidding? We're starting now. Drive fast. Actually, don't drive fast, drive safe, because we need you for all the work that's coming our way."

He smiled. "I'll see you soon." He hit Liz's number next. The call went immediately to voice mail.

"Lizzie, I need to talk to you. I know I'm not your favorite person right now, but call me back. We said we weren't going to let the results of our competition change things between us. I don't want to turn us into liars. Do you?"

Chapter Sixteen

Liz listened to Michael's message as she got out of her car and walked up the steps to her parent's house. She didn't want to be a liar, but she wasn't ready to call him back yet. She had something important to do first. Actually, she had two things to do, and she was quite certain that the first would be the most difficult.

She found her dad in the family room. He was reading a book, his glasses sliding down the bridge of his nose as he raised his gaze to hers. She didn't know where her mom was, but it was probably better that she talk to her dad alone.

"You're spoiling me, Liz," he said. "Three times in one week."

She kissed him on the cheek and sat down on the couch. "How are you feeling?"

"Like I wish that didn't always have to be your first question."

"Sorry. I know you get tired of people asking."

"I appreciate the concern, but I'm feeling better. I know it probably looks to you like I spend all my time in this chair, but your mother and I made it around six blocks earlier today, so I got my exercise."

"I'm glad you're out walking again."

"Of course I have to listen to your mother go on and on about how she wants to redo the garden based on all the other yards in the neighborhood."

"Of course," she echoed, as they exchanged a smile.

"But now that we have my health out of the way, should I assume this has to do with work?"

"It does. I just drove back from Playworld, and I didn't get the account. I'm sorry."

"Why are you apologizing? I'm sure you did your best."

"I did. And I would have had the account if Brian hadn't called Mr. Hayward and tried to throw his weight around. Charlie Hayward is a very smart man, and he quickly realized that I didn't have the firm's support. He was right, I don't have anyone's support. They want me gone, Dad."

He sighed. "I know. You've been fighting so hard, and I should have told you a long time ago to stop. It was my fault. After they moved your office and stripped away some of your accounts, I knew what was happening, but I didn't want them to win, so I let you keep battling, but the truth is they won when I left."

Hearing her dad talk, she had a feeling she knew exactly where her competitive will to win came from. "The truth is that they lost when you left. Charlie told me he asked for me because he respected your record and he figured you'd taught me right, and you had. He didn't want Damien, Falks and now Hargrove; he wanted us, you and me."

"I wish we could have had our own company, Liz. I just wasn't counting on getting sick and having to retire so early." He paused, giving her a long look. "But that's the way things ended up. You need to live your life, honey. And I don't want you to ever think that you let me down. I'm the one who let you down by trying to get you to finish my fight. That wasn't fair. I had my life."

"Don't talk like it's over," she interrupted.

"I didn't mean it that way. I don't know what's coming my way, but I do know that my career is done. I'm retired now, and I'm going to start enjoying things instead of wishing I could have my old life back. I had a great run in PR. Maybe you will, too. Or perhaps you'll decide to do something else. But whatever you decide, I want you to pick for yourself and not for me."

A tear dripped out of her eye and she hastily wiped it away, knowing her dad hated to see her cry. "Thanks, Dad. You know I love you."

"I love you, too. And I'm planning to stick around for a long while. I want to walk you down the aisle, Lizzie."

"Then you're really going to have to stick around for a long time," she said with a watery smile.

He grinned. "I don't think it's going to be that long. I saw the way you looked at Michael; the way he looked at you."

"He beat me again," she said.

"Then maybe it's time you ended up on the same side."

"You sound just like him." She got to her feet. "I'm going to the office now—to hand in my resignation."

"Don't give 'em two weeks. They don't deserve it."

"You're right. They don't. But I probably will, because my dad taught me how to be a professional."

He tipped his head. "You're my girl."

"Always," she said, blowing him a kiss as she left the room.

* * *

The party at Michael's firm was going into its third hour with most of the staff well on their way to a good buzz. Michael left the celebration for a moment and stepped into his office to check his phone. He was hoping to see a message or a missed call from Liz. It was almost seven. Where the hell was she and why wasn't she calling him back? He tried her number again, but once more it went straight to voicemail.

"Come on, Liz, just call me back." He hung up the phone, not knowing what else to say.

"Why are you frowning?" Erica asked, coming into his office.

"I'm not."

She gave him that big sisterly look that said she knew he was lying. "It's Liz, isn't it?"

"She hasn't called me back."

"She just needs time to regroup, Michael."

"Or I'm never going to hear from her again," he countered, sitting down in his chair.

Erica perched on the corner of his desk. "She's always made you a little crazy, but this time around I think you know it's more than crazy; it's love."

He frowned. "I'm not talking to you about this."

"Why not? I'm your big sis and your boss. I could order you to talk to me about it."

"You're drunk."

"Not yet, but getting there," she said with a grin. "This is the biggest night we've ever had."

"I know. It's great."

She made a face at him. "You could sound a little more enthusiastic."

"I am happy for you."

"For us, Michael."

"About that, Erica."

"Wait a second," she said, standing back up straight. "You are not going to tell me you're quitting."

"I'm not quitting."

Relief flashed in her eyes. "Okay, good. You had me worried for a second."

"But I am going to cut back my hours."

"What are you talking about? We just got a huge account."

"You and Kent are the brains of this operation, I'm the beauty," he said dryly.

"Very funny. You're more than that. You brought this account in, and Charlie Hayward wants to work with you."

"And he will. I'll do everything I can for Playworld, but I also want to do something on the side. I've been offered an assistant coaching position with the Blackhawks."

Her jaw dropped. "Are you serious? I thought you couldn't even stand to hear the word football."

"I realize now that I acted too hastily. I told the team that I could give them ten hours a week, and they accepted. It's more of a consulting job than anything else. And I don't know how long it will last, but those guys playing right now are still my guys. I want to see them do well. But I don't want to let you down, Erica. I think I can do both."

"I think you can, too. In the end, if football calls you back, then you should go. You have to live your own dream. Just don't go before Charlie signs the contracts." She paused. "We'll have to tell him, too. It wouldn't be ethical not to."

"Of course. I don't think it will make a difference. Charlie knows you did the work. I told him that. He wants me for my celebrity contacts, and he'll still have that. I'm not going to let either one of you down."

"I believe you. Come back to the party."

"In a minute. I'm going to try Liz again."

"Haven't you already left her a half dozen messages? Do you want her to think you're stalking her?"

"If it gets her to call me back, then I don't really care."

"Michael," Liz said.

His gaze swung to the door and a wave of relief ran through him.

"I didn't call you back because I wanted to talk to you in

person." Liz looked at Erica. "You're Michael's sister. I remember you from high school."

"Good memory," Erica said. "I remember you, too, but mostly because Michael always complained about you."

"I'm sure he did a lot of complaining after I broke his nose."

"What?" Erica shot him a look. "*She* broke your nose? You said it was some guy on the football team."

"I wasn't going to tell you it was a girl."

"Well, I would love to hear that story, but I'm thinking you two need to talk."

"Congratulations," Liz said. "I know your firm is going to do great things for Playworld."

"I really thought it was going to be your firm," Erica said.

"Well, it's not my firm anymore."

"Really?" Erica asked. "What does that mean?"

"I quit today. I told the partners I could not work with a company who didn't understand how valuable I was. I offered two weeks notice, and they told me to leave immediately, which I was very happy to do. So I'm done."

"I can't believe it," he said. He'd been thinking she should quit; he just hadn't believed she'd actually do it.

"I'm going to go back to the party," Erica interrupted. "Come out and have a drink when you're done in here."

"I will, I could use a drink," Liz said.

Erica moved past Liz, then paused. "When you start looking for a new job, maybe think of us. We're about to get an influx of cash from a really big client, who I think is also quite a fan of yours. Just think about it."

"Look at that, you quit a job and get an offer an hour later," Michael said.

"I don't think she meant that," Liz said.

"Oh, I'm quite sure she did. But you don't have to think about that now."

"I literally can't. My head is spinning."

He walked around his desk and put his arms around her. He buried his face in her hair and breathed in her sweet scent and realized how worried he'd been that he would never have this opportunity again. He lifted his head and looked into her eyes. "You scared me with your silence. Why didn't you call me back?"

"I wanted to take care of some things first."

"Did you talk to your dad?"

She nodded, giving him a teary-eyed smile. "He was really understanding about it all. He actually apologized to me, saying he knew I was fighting for him, and he should have told me to let go a long time ago."

"I'm glad it went so well. How do you feel?"

"Like I lost fifty pounds."

He pulled her close and gave her another kiss, then had to ask. "How do you feel about me beating you again?"

"It wasn't fun hearing Charlie give you the account, but it was the right decision."

"Charlie would be thrilled if you came to work for us."

"I'm sure your sister doesn't need my help."

"Oh, she does, believe me, especially since I just told her I'm going to be working part-time."

Liz raised her eyebrow. "The coaching job?"

"Yeah. I told Hank I could give them ten hours a week for the rest of the season. I'll be watching a lot of film, working from here, of course, although I'll probably fly out to the games. I think I can do both, at least for awhile."

"Oh, Michael. I'm so glad. I think it's the right move."

"Me, too. I'm getting my life back on track."

"We both are."

"Yes, but I have to admit that ten minutes ago, my track looked pretty lonely, and I realized that neither Playworld nor football was going to make me really happy. I need you for that." He paused as he gazed into her eyes. "I'm in love with you, Lizzie. I think I have been since I was fifteen years old. I just couldn't get it right until now." He licked his lips. "Tell me I got it right, and I'm not about to get another fist to the face?"

She smiled and ran her hand down his cheek. "I would never want to hurt this face again. I'm in love with you, too, Michael."

His heart jumped into his throat. He felt like he'd just won the Super Bowl.

"My dad told me that maybe you and I should start playing for the same side. I'm thinking he's right," she said.

"I'm thinking your father is a very smart man."

"He is. So are you. You stole my heart a long time ago. I think the only way I'm going to get it back is to be with you."

"I like that idea. I think we should spend the rest of our lives together."

"Whoa," she said abruptly. "You don't have to propose right this second."

"I'm not. You'll know when I'm proposing. I just want you to know that I'm in this forever, and I am going to meet you at the front of a church one day. That's a promise."

Her eyes filled with happiness. "I'm glad, because I did catch that damn wedding bouquet."

He laughed. "That's right. Why do I have the feeling we're going to have a big wedding?"

"Because we are." Her gaze turned serious. "But, really I'm not trying to rush you into anything, Michael. It's been a crazy day and it's all happening really fast."

"It's not fast. We've been slowly inching our way toward this moment for nine years. We weren't ready for each other before. We are now. And just so you know. You stole my heart, too."

"I love you, Michael."

She pressed her hands against his chest and raised her sweet mouth to his.

"I love you, too," he murmured.

Epilogue

Valentine's Day

"I can't believe another one of us is getting married," Liz said, meeting Julie's gaze in the dressing room mirror at the Four Seasons Hotel where Andrea was about to get married.

Julie couldn't quite believe it, either. First Laurel got married, now it was Andrea, and Liz was probably next. She was happy for all of them, but she was starting to feel like the love train had left the station without her. Not that she was that interested in getting on board. Well, maybe she was a little interested, because seeing her friends in love had made her think that maybe her own past experiences were exceptions to the rule and not the actual rule.

"When do you think Michael is going to propose?" she asked Liz.

Liz gave her a secretive smile. "I have a feeling it might be later tonight, but I'm not sure. He's been really mysterious lately."

"Well, it is about time for us to start planning another wedding," she said with a laugh. "I still sometimes can't believe that you and the high school quarterback are in love."

"It was a dream I never thought would come true," Liz

admitted. "Do you remember all those nights in college when we stayed up late talking about our dream guys? I think it was always Michael for me. I just never thought I could actually get him."

"But you did."

"What about you, Julie?"

"Me? Those dream guys never had faces or names. I don't think I've met *the one* yet."

"It usually happens when you least expect it. I certainly never thought a PR pitch would lead the way to love."

"Speaking of work, how do you like working for Michael's sister?"

"I love it. Erica and I have similar approaches to business, and she totally respects my experience and my ideas. Charlie Hayward is thrilled that we're both on the Playworld account, and Michael is happy to be the front man. He uses his connections when he has to, but now he also has time to do some coaching. So it all worked out perfectly." She turned around to face Julie. "I can't quite believe how happy I am. Sometimes I feel like pinching myself to make sure I'm not dreaming."

"You're not dreaming, and you deserve to be this happy, even if it does make me a little jealous."

"Well, we have to find you a man next."

She laughed. "I think we have enough brides-to-be at the moment." As she finished speaking, Andrea came through the door in her wedding dress, her beautiful blonde hair swept up in a pretty, loose knot on top of her head. Her sister Laurel, followed, careful to pick up Andrea's train so she didn't trip on it. They were followed by the rest of the bridesmaids: Maggie, Jessica, Isabella and Kate, who was once again doubling as bridesmaid and wedding planner.

"Let's make a toast to Andrea," Kate said, as she and Isabella handed out glasses of champagne. "Liz, do you want

Book List

The Callaway Family Series
#1 On A Night Like This
#2 So This Is Love
#3 Falling For A Stranger
#4 Between Now And Forever
#5 All A Heart Needs
#6 That Summer Night
#7 When Shadows Fall

Nobody But You (A Callaway Wedding Novella)

The Wish Series
#1 A Secret Wish
#2 Just A Wish Away
#3 When Wishes Collide

Almost Home
All She Ever Wanted
Ask Mariah
Daniel's Gift
Don't Say A Word
Golden Lies
Just The Way You Are
Love Will Find A Way
One True Love
Ryan's Return
Some Kind of Wonderful
Summer Secrets
The Sweetest Thing

The Sanders Brothers Series
#1 Silent Run
#2 Silent Fall

The Deception Series
#1 Taken
#2 Played

to do the honors?"

"To Andrea," Liz said, lifting her glass. "May you and Alex always be as happy as you are today."

"Thanks Liz," Andrea said as they toasted to her future. "I'm sure you and Michael will be the next to get married, so I may have to aim my bouquet at someone else." She eyed her bridesmaids. "Who is feeling lucky?"

All the single girls raised their hands and then looked at each other and started to laugh.

"If you married or almost engaged women want to keep this wedding train going, you better get your husbands and fiancés to come up with some single, good-looking friends," Maggie said, giving Andrea, Laurel and Liz a pointed look. "Don't leave us hanging."

Julie laughed and raised her glass in the air. "I'll drink to that."

They clinked their glasses together and toasted to happy days ahead—for all of them.

THE END

Dear Reader,

I hope you're enjoying the Bachelors and Bridesmaids Se
It's really fun to give each of the bridesmaids their own sp
love story, and I had a great time getting Liz and Micha
fall in love.

The next story features Julie Michaels, charity fundraiser
has to deal with some emotional baggage in her past or
way to finding Mr. Right. ALL YOUR LOVING will be
December 18, 2014.

The first book in the series, KISS ME FOREVER, is
available. That story features Andrea and her sexy billion
Alex Donovan.

Happy Reading!

Barbara

About The Author

Barbara Freethy is a #1 New York Times Bestselling Author of 41 novels ranging from contemporary romance to romantic suspense and women's fiction. Traditionally published for many years, Barbara opened her own publishing company in 2011 and has since sold over 4.8 million ebooks! Nineteen of her titles have appeared on the New York Times and USA Today Bestseller Lists.

Known for her emotional and compelling stories of love, family, mystery and romance, Barbara enjoys writing about ordinary people caught up in extraordinary adventures. She is currently writing a connected family series, The Callaways, which includes: ON A NIGHT LIKE THIS (#1), SO THIS IS LOVE (#2), FALLING FOR A STRANGER (#3) BETWEEN NOW AND FOREVER (#4), ALL A HEART NEEDS (#5), THAT SUMMER NIGHT (#6) and WHEN SHADOWS FALL (#7). If you love series with romance, suspense and a little adventure, you'll love the Callaways.

Barbara also recently released the WISH SERIES, a series of books connected by the theme of wishes including: A SECRET WISH (#1), JUST A WISH AWAY (#2) and WHEN WISHES COLLIDE (#3).

Other popular standalone titles include: DON'T SAY A WORD, SILENT RUN, SILENT FALL, and RYAN'S RETURN.

Barbara's books have won numerous awards - she is a six-time finalist for the RITA for best contemporary romance from Romance Writers of America and a two-time winner for DANIEL'S GIFT and THE WAY BACK HOME.

Barbara has lived all over the state of California and currently resides in Northern California where she draws much of her inspiration from the beautiful bay area.

For a complete listing of books, as well as excerpts and contests, and to connect with Barbara:

Visit Barbara's Website:
www.barbarafreethy.com
Join Barbara on Facebook:
www.facebook.com/barbarafreethybooks
Follow Barbara on Twitter:
www.twitter.com/barbarafreethy

21979173R00098

Made in the USA
San Bernardino, CA
15 June 2015

to do the honors?"

"To Andrea," Liz said, lifting her glass. "May you and Alex always be as happy as you are today."

"Thanks Liz," Andrea said as they toasted to her future. "I'm sure you and Michael will be the next to get married, so I may have to aim my bouquet at someone else." She eyed her bridesmaids. "Who is feeling lucky?"

All the single girls raised their hands and then looked at each other and started to laugh.

"If you married or almost engaged women want to keep this wedding train going, you better get your husbands and fiancés to come up with some single, good-looking friends," Maggie said, giving Andrea, Laurel and Liz a pointed look. "Don't leave us hanging."

Julie laughed and raised her glass in the air. "I'll drink to that."

They clinked their glasses together and toasted to happy days ahead—for all of them.

THE END

Dear Reader,

I hope you're enjoying the Bachelors and Bridesmaids Series. It's really fun to give each of the bridesmaids their own special love story, and I had a great time getting Liz and Michael to fall in love.

The next story features Julie Michaels, charity fundraiser who has to deal with some emotional baggage in her past on the way to finding Mr. Right. ALL YOUR LOVING will be out December 18, 2014.

The first book in the series, KISS ME FOREVER, is also available. That story features Andrea and her sexy billionaire Alex Donovan.

Happy Reading!

Barbara

Book List

The Callaway Family Series
#1 On A Night Like This
#2 So This Is Love
#3 Falling For A Stranger
#4 Between Now And Forever
#5 All A Heart Needs
#6 That Summer Night
#7 When Shadows Fall

Nobody But You (A Callaway Wedding Novella)

The Wish Series
#1 A Secret Wish
#2 Just A Wish Away
#3 When Wishes Collide

Almost Home
All She Ever Wanted
Ask Mariah
Daniel's Gift
Don't Say A Word
Golden Lies
Just The Way You Are
Love Will Find A Way
One True Love
Ryan's Return
Some Kind of Wonderful
Summer Secrets
The Sweetest Thing

The Sanders Brothers Series
#1 Silent Run
#2 Silent Fall

The Deception Series
#1 Taken
#2 Played